LAUGHING AT THE THUNDER

The War Brides Trilogy:
Book Three

Other books by Amanda Harte:

The *War Brides* Trilogy:
Dancing in the Rain
Whistling in the Dark

The *Unwanted Legacies* Series:
Imperfect Together
Strings Attached

Moonlight Masquerade

LAUGHING AT THE THUNDER

•

Amanda Harte

AVALON BOOKS
NEW YORK

PRINTED IN THE UNITED STATES OF AMERICA
ON ACID-FREE PAPER
BY HADDON CRAFTSMEN, BLOOMSBURG, PENNSYLVANIA

For Kathryn M. Krouse,
a modern day heroine.

Acknowledgments

Although writing is, for the most part, a solitary profession, I couldn't have written the *War Brides Trilogy* without the help of a number of people. I'd like to thank:

Colleen Byrne, Assistant Director and Reference Librarian at the New Providence Memorial Library, who has been invaluable in researching so many books and who provided me with countless sources of information for the trilogy, including the George Eastman House.

Todd Gustavson, Curator of Technology for the George Eastman House, for generously sharing his knowledge of early 20th century photography and for introducing me to the Press Graflex. Any technical errors are mine, not Todd's.

Elisabeth Madden, for helping me with the German phrases. I hope I got the umlauts in the right places, Liz.

Erin Cartwright-Niumata, my editor, who convinced me that it would be fun to write a World War I trilogy.

My heartfelt thanks to all of you!

Chapter One

April 1918

He doubted he'd find her here. Tom Fleming drummed his fingers on the steering wheel as he stared at the modest sign that welcomed him to Canela, Texas. The excitement that had accompanied him when he'd begun the trip had evaporated along with the sense of anticipation that entering each new village had once brought him. Now all that was left was ennui, a most unwelcome companion.

Tom slowed the automobile and looked around. The town appeared to have some appeal. Those live oaks with Spanish moss dripping from the lower branches were attractive enough. And, while he didn't necessarily believe it, Canela's slogan intrigued him. Even a cynic like Tom couldn't help wondering just what the inhabitants of a town that proclaimed itself to be "The Friendliest Little Town in East Texas" thought made them so special. Did they throw garlands of moss around visitors, the way Hawaiian Islanders greeted visitors with leis? Or did they offer passersby fragrant tea in cups so fragile a man was convinced they'd shatter into tiny shards if he so much as breathed on them?

1

Tom let out the clutch and urged the Model T forward. He had come this far; he might as well see what Canela had to offer. If she wasn't here—which he suspected was the case—perhaps he'd find something that would placate Sidney for a week or two.

Taking a deep breath, Tom forced himself to focus on the road. That was better than thinking about Sidney and the way they had parted. Sidney was a man of doubts. For Pete's sake, he was an editor. That meant he was paid to have doubts. Tom knew that. The problem was, though he'd never in a million years admit it to the man, he was starting to share Sidney's doubts. And that was bad. It was worse than bad. It was horrible. Doubts could wreck a man's concentration; they could destroy his creativity. And if there was one thing Tom did not need, it was anything that would damage his artistic senses. He couldn't afford that any more than he could afford to let this dry spell continue.

Pedestrian. Ordinary. Dull. No matter what Sidney said, Tom's work was not dull. It was brilliant. It was inspired. It was . . . Tom cringed. There was no sense in pretending. The last few months had not been his best. That was why, though a year ago every newspaper in the country had clamored for a photograph by Tom Fleming, now only Sidney would consider his submissions, and then with caveats. Sidney had minced no words when he told Tom the most he'd agree to do was look at his prints. The days of guaranteed sales were gone. But all that would change the minute he found *her*.

Tom depressed the accelerator, anxious to reach the center of this allegedly friendly town. She would be here. She had to be, for time was running out. He had to deliver what he'd promised, and he had to do it soon. Otherwise . . . He wouldn't think about that.

Tom slowed the car again at what was obviously the heart of Canela. The street was wider than he'd expected, the spacious homes that had graced the previous two blocks giving way to a dozen or more small shops, each boasting a different colored awning, though the buildings themselves were all painted the same shade of white. There were no live oaks or pecan trees lining the street here, and the afternoon sun felt uncomfortably warm beating on his shoulders. If he didn't find her here, he'd put the Model T's top up before he continued to the next town.

As two young women exited one of the stores, Tom slowed the car even more. Perhaps one of them was the woman he sought. But a quick look told him that, though they were young and attractive, neither was the special someone who had taken him so far from home, the woman he had sought in both big cities and small towns, the one Sidney was certain existed only in Tom's imagination.

She wasn't a figment! She wasn't simply a face that haunted his dreams and kept him driving far too late each day. She was real. All Tom had to do was find her. And when he did, everything would be right again. The dry spell would be over. What had once been described as "Tom Fleming's infallible eye" would return. Tom would have his picture, and hundreds—no, thousands—of men would have something to believe in. It would happen. Tom knew that. All he had to do was find her.

"I want to do something different for Independence Day." Martha Wentworth York dipped a rag into the pail and began to clean the chalkboard. Though it was unseasonably warm for April, the well water was cool, reminding Martha of the spring when it had been Henry and not one of the students who had brought the buckets of water and Henry, not a plump middle-aged woman with a coronet of blond braids, who helped her. That had been five years ago, when hardly anyone in Canela had heard of a town called Sarajevo and no one had dreamed that war would change their lives.

On the other side of the classroom, Martha's assistant cupped her hand around one ear. "Could you repeat that?

I think my ears have been playing tricks on me. If I didn't know better, I would have said that the woman who abhors change more than anyone I've ever met just suggested breaking with tradition."

Anna Gottlieb's mockingly serious words dispelled Martha's gloom, and she laughed. "Now, Anna, I'm not that bad."

"You aren't?" The woman who was old enough to be Martha's mother fisted her hands on her hips. "Tell me who else in Canela knows exactly where each ornament was placed on the town's Christmas tree for the last ten years and just how to fold the bunting to make the mayor's parade float look identical to the one the very first mayor of Canela rode?"

Martha climbed onto the step stool. There were times—and this was one of them—when she regretted her small stature. Anna was tall for a woman, and when she wrote on the chalkboard, she frequently forgot that Martha was only 5'3" and that the schoolchildren were even shorter.

"The tree and the float are traditions," Martha insisted as she swabbed the top of the board. "It's important to maintain tradition."

"I'm not arguing with you. I just said that I was surprised when you suggested another change."

"Another? What was the first one?"

"Letting the pupils leave early today."

Martha shrugged as she climbed down from the stool. "It's such a beautiful day that I wanted them to enjoy it." She frowned at the chalkboard. "I'll admit that washing this isn't my favorite way to spend an afternoon, but I remember what a treat it was to get out of school early. Since I wanted to be outside today, I figured that the children would enjoy the extra free time." And maybe the mundane act of cleaning the schoolroom would keep her from thinking about Henry and dreams that would never come true.

"I'm sure the children are having fun right now," Anna

agreed as she straightened the front row of desks, "but what about you?"

Martha's hand stopped in mid-stroke. "What about me?"

"Are you having fun?"

It was an absurd question. Fun was something an adult rarely thought about these days. "As much as anyone," she said at last.

Anna stared at her for a long moment, then shrugged her ample shoulders. "Back to your original comment: is the reason you're looking for something different for the celebration the fact that we aren't having fireworks this year?"

Martha nodded, relieved by the change of subject. "That's part of it. I understand why the Town Council doesn't want anything that sounds like artillery fire, but depriving the children of a special holiday seems to me to be a bit like last year's crazy plan to eliminate gift giving at Christmas. It's not going to stop the war or even shorten it."

"Perhaps the war will be over by July."

Martha wrung out the rag and cleaned the last section of the board. The day was warm and beautiful, a light breeze wafting the fresh scents of spring through the open window. Though it was a day to savor life, halfway around the world, men were killing one another, the way they'd been doing for almost four years, the way some thought they'd do for the rest of eternity. "Oh, Anna, I wish I could believe that the war would end before July, but I'm afraid that I can't. All I hope now is that this really is the War to End All Wars and that when it's finally over, it's the very last one."

Anna looked up from the books that she was straightening. "The war has affected you more than most of us in Canela." She looked pointedly at Martha's left hand and the narrow gold band that still decorated her third finger, though she had been a widow for over three years.

Martha closed her eyes for a second, thinking of her

husband, who would never return, and her siblings, now so far away. Carolyn had gone to France as a nurse when her fiancé joined the Army, and Emily had wrangled her way across the ocean, allegedly to serve as an ambulance driver. Only Martha knew that the real reason Emily had gone to the war zone was that she refused to believe that their brother Theo had been killed along with the rest of his battalion. Emily had insisted that there was no need to put a second gold star in their front window, for Theo, she claimed, was still alive. She would prove it. If anyone could find Theo, it was Emily, and Martha prayed that her sister would be successful. But in the meantime, she was alone, the only one of the four Wentworth children still in Canela.

"The evenings are lonely," she admitted. "That's one of the reasons I'm thankful I'm teaching. The children remind me of what's important." Their antics filled her days, and knowing that they were waiting for her gave Martha a reason to get out of bed each morning.

"I agree." Anna stared out the window for a moment. When she turned and faced Martha again, her face was somber. "I wish I could stop worrying about my cousins."

Anna's cousins were still in Germany, fighting on the opposite side of this terrible war. Though Anna said little, Martha knew that her friend wondered whether Hans or Georg would kill—or be killed by—someone from her adopted hometown. Martha's heart went out to her friend. Anna was now an American citizen and as loyal to the country as anyone Martha knew, but she still had ties to Germany. Family was family, no matter which flag they saluted.

"Do you have any ideas for Independence Day?" Martha asked, deliberately changing the subject.

An hour later, she flung up her hands in surrender. "We're not getting anywhere." Though she and Anna had considered a dozen or more different ideas for adding to the holiday festivities, none of them had sparked Martha's imagination enough for her to pursue it. "Maybe we'll do better tomorrow when we're feeling fresh," she said as she and Anna left the school, heading in opposite directions. *Or maybe,* Martha added silently as she turned onto Oak Street, *walking will inspire me.* Her family had joked that she did her best thinking when ambulatory, claiming that if the girls were perplexed, Carolyn would be admonished to put on her thinking cap, while Martha was told to don her walking shoes. She couldn't explain it; all she knew was that the simple act of putting one foot in front of the other sometimes helped to clear her thoughts.

This afternoon, however, inspiration proved elusive. Instead of thinking about the children's celebration or reveling in the beauty of a Texas spring, Martha's thoughts revolved around her brother and sisters. A year ago, they'd all been here in Canela, and the war—though it had raged for almost three years—had seemed distant. It was true that the conflict had taken Henry. Though America did not join the warring forces until the spring of 1917, Martha's husband had enlisted in the Canadian Air Force along with his cousins the week that Canada had declared its support for the English and French. Before 1914 ended, Martha had received a telegram, telling her that Henry's plane had been shot down and that her husband was buried in a place she could barely pronounce.

The war had come to Canela, and yet even then, for most of the residents it had seemed as if it were someone else's war. All that had changed the day President Wilson declared that the United States could tolerate the killing no longer. Within months, it seemed that every able-bodied man in Canela had joined the Army. Blue stars, indicating that a member of the household was serving in the armed forces, appeared in many front windows. Only Martha's also had a gold star, visible proof that Henry had paid the ultimate price to make the world safe again.

Theo had been one of the first to enlist. Martha had expected that. Her brother was the most patriotic person she knew. What she hadn't anticipated was her sisters leaving. Their reasons were valid. It was just that. . . . Martha took a deep breath, trying to control her emotions. Perhaps Anna was right. Perhaps she didn't like change. Martha nodded slowly. There was no "perhaps" about it. When change involved loved ones leaving, she didn't like it. Not one bit.

Henry had left. Though he'd been confident he'd be back in a few months, he had never returned. When Theo had left, they'd known it would be for more than a few months, but they'd all believed that Theo—"lucky Theo" as his friends had called him—would return. If the U.S. Army was correct, he would not. Even her sisters' departures, which were expected to be only temporary, had taken unexpected directions. It appeared that neither Carolyn nor Emily would return to Canela when the war ended. There was no doubt about it. Martha did not like change, for change seemed to deprive her of the ones she loved most.

Martha quickened her pace, anxious to reach home. She would feel better there, and maybe if she was lucky something there would trigger an idea for the Independence Day celebration. As she turned onto Broad Street, Martha heard the unmistakable but surprising sound of an automobile. With all the wartime restrictions, fewer people drove during the week, preferring to save their gasoline for special visits on Saturdays. Sundays, which had once been the favorite day for pleasure drives, had become "gasless," just as Mondays and Wednesdays were "wheatless."

She turned, curious about who was out driving. The car looked like all of Henry Ford's creations. It was tall and black, and although she knew that her sister Emily would be able to tell which year it had been made, to Martha it appeared the same as every other Model T. The top was down. That was not unusual. On beautiful spring days, most drivers would want to enjoy the fresh air.

What was unusual was the driver. He was a stranger. Cars might be rare in Canela. Strangers were even rarer, and handsome, male strangers were virtually unheard of. Martha could not remember the last time one of that species had entered the town. Conscious that she was staring, she turned and continued to walk, deliberately focusing her attention on the stores she was passing. There was no point in remembering that the stranger had golden blond hair and a face that could easily have starred in a film. She didn't need to recall that his shoulders were broad, and that he held his head as if he were a man who was supremely confident in his own abilities.

She certainly had no reason to speculate on why he was here. Film-star-handsome men did not come to Canela. If he really was a star, he ought to be in Hollywood, making movies like *The Beast of Berlin* to help with the war effort. And if he wasn't a star, shouldn't he be on the Western Front along with Theo and the rest of the male population of Canela? The only men who remained were either too old to fight or had some disability. The stranger appeared to fit neither category.

He was simply passing through town, Martha told herself. But when the car seemed to slow, almost as if it were matching her pace, her curiosity prevailed and she turned around again. This time the stranger flashed her a smile that surely belonged on a film screen. Though her sister Carolyn claimed that her new husband was the most handsome man on earth, and little Emily's letters were filled with news of a man she'd met in Calais, a man she vowed was so handsome he could almost be called beautiful, Martha knew that neither of those men could compare to the stranger in the Model T. He was truly breathtaking. His smile was so warm, so inviting, that it literally stole her breath.

It was absurd. She was Martha, the sensible Wentworth daughter. She was the girl who had fallen in love with the boy down the street when she was eight years old and never fell out of love with him. She was not—she most definitely was not—the kind of woman who swooned at the sight of a handsome man. So, why on earth did her face feel as if it were on fire, and why were her hands clutching her bag as if the handles were a lifeline and she a drowning sailor?

It was ridiculous. Spring fever must have addled her brain. That was the only reason she imagined that the man in the Model T was following her. That was the only reason she was deluded enough to believe that a man so handsome that he ought to be in Hollywood wanted to speak to her. That was the only reason why his smile made her feel as if they had met before and were renewing their acquaintance.

There was only one thing to do. Martha quickened her pace and turned onto Main Street. Undoubtedly the stranger would continue down Broad. But he did not. Behind her, Martha heard the car turn, then accelerate. She would not run. Of course she would not. That would be unseemly. Instead, Martha walked as quickly as she could without drawing undue attention to herself. Mr. Martin's shop would be open. She would enter it. And then the man would continue to drive down Main Street. He was simply passing through Canela. That was all.

Seconds later, Martha gave the shopkeeper a hasty greeting and hurried to the back of the store. It might be cowardly, but she felt safer there, away from the blond stranger's all-too-disturbing gaze. Here, her pulse could return to normal and that distressing flush would fade from her cheeks.

Martha took a deep breath and feigned interest in the latest issue of the *Texas Courier*. It mattered naught that she had already read it from cover to cover.

The door opened. She did not look up. Of course it wasn't the stranger. By now, he was on the other side of town, headed for San Antonio or wherever it was he was going.

She heard footsteps and Mr. Martin's greeting, but still she did not look up. There was no reason to greet everyone who entered the shop. It wouldn't be the stranger. And, even if it were, it wasn't as if he were coming to see her. No one went out of his way to visit Martha York.

The steps came closer. Martha turned another page in the magazine. Wasn't it interesting that the experts claimed the bluebonnets would be more beautiful this year than they'd been in the past decade? Yes, indeed, that was fascinating. Far more fascinating than the sound of unfamiliar boots on the floor.

The footsteps turned the corner, then stopped. For a second, there was silence. And then he spoke. "You're perfect!"

Chapter Two

He'd found her! The rush of excitement that raced through his blood and set his nerve endings to tingling was unlike anything Tom had ever experienced. Even the day he'd heard the thunder hadn't felt like this. It had started when he had seen her walking down the street. Though at first all he saw was her back, there was something about her that drew him, that told him she was the one. It wasn't simply her sweet curves and the silver-blond hair that swung as she walked. It wasn't simply the way she held her head and shoulders, her posture almost militarily alert, yet managing to appear soft at the same time. It was everything combined, the whole package.

Then he saw her face. Tom gripped the steering wheel, trying to control his elation. Was it only five minutes earlier that he'd been convinced Canela had nothing to offer? This was one time Tom was happy to be proven wrong. His fingers itched to hold the Graflex, to begin composing the picture.

She had obviously heard the car and turned to see who was following her. If Tom had had any doubts that she was the woman he'd sought for so long, they would have evaporated at the sight of her face. She wasn't beautiful in the way that a film star was. Though others had raved over the appearance of women like Theda Bara and Mary Pickford, Tom had never found them attractive. Those women had superficial beauty. What he saw in this woman was something deeper and far more alluring.

Just as her posture had suggested both firmness and softness at the same time, there was something about this woman's expression that told him her confidence was tempered by vulnerability. It was an intriguing combination and one that he knew instinctively would appeal to his readers. When a man looked at this woman, he would see not just a beautiful face but also the heart behind that face.

Though he knew he was grinning foolishly, Tom couldn't help it. Relief and exhilaration surged through him. He had found her! Sidney was wrong. His own doubts had been wrong. This wasn't a foolish quest. The Fourth of July Woman was real, and Tom had found her here in the Friendliest Little Town in East Texas. What a glorious day this had turned out to be!

She was moving more quickly now, a woman with a purpose. Tom debated his course of action. He could call out to her and ask her to stop, but that seemed rude. She deserved more courtesy than that. When she entered one of the shops with the brightly colored awnings, Tom knew she had made his job easier. He stopped the car and leaped out. Then, reminding himself that this was a small town and there were undoubtedly people watching him, he forced himself to walk toward the store. Perhaps no one would notice that his strides were longer than normal, making his pace almost as fast as a run.

He gave the shopkeeper a perfunctory greeting, then looked around. It was an ordinary general store, little different from any of the dozens of stores he'd entered on his travels. The shelves held the same merchandise he'd seen in Madison and Memphis and Monterey. The items were even displayed in much the same order. There was nothing special about it, except . . . Tom's eyes scanned the room, searching for her. There she was—standing in the last aisle, that silvery blond head bent over some sort of newspaper. He strode toward her.

"You're perfect!" The words slipped out, seemingly without volition.

She looked up, her eyes wide with surprise. "I beg your pardon."

Tom took a deep breath, trying to control his own surprise. He'd known she was petite, only a few inches over five feet. He'd known she was graceful. He'd known so much, but he hadn't known this. Though he hadn't been close enough to see them, he'd assumed that her eyes were blue. What surprised him was that they were almost the same shade as the turquoises he had seen being polished in Santa Fe. For the first time, Tom wished that he were a painter. If he were, he could capture this woman's extraordinary beauty in color. As it was, he was limited to black and white and shades of gray.

"I'm sorry." For so many things, not the least of which was his inability to record the brilliance of those lovely eyes. "My mother taught me better manners. It's just that I've been looking for you for so long."

The woman took a step backward, her fingers clutching the magazine. She wore a dark gray skirt that grazed the tops of her high-button shoes, a simple white shirtwaist, and and one of those ridiculous concoctions that women called hats. The clothing was ordinary; the woman was not. Unfortunately, it seemed that with each word he spoke, Tom drove her further away. That was not what he intended, not at all.

"Is this man bothering you, Martha?" The shopkeeper appeared at Tom's side, his posture clearly stating that he was prepared to defend the woman he called Martha.

"I'm sure he has a logical explanation, Mr. Martin." Martha's voice was low and tinged with what appeared to be mild amusement. She had relaxed visibly when the shop-keeper had come to the back of the store. "He's obviously mistaken me for someone else."

"My apologies, Miss . . ." Tom let his words trail off, hoping she would tell him the rest of her name. Though he'd already begun to think of her as Martha, the Fourth of July Woman, he could not address her that way. Not yet. He needed her to tell him her last name.

She did. And when she did, Tom felt as if someone had punched him in the stomach.

"I'm Mrs. York."

She was married. Tom hoped his dismay wasn't obvious. He hadn't expected that. In all the time that he had been searching for the Fourth of July Woman, he had never once considered that she would be married. He had known she would be young, but not too young, and beautiful—but not too beautiful. Though he had never vocalized the thought, he had also believed that she would be single. And she wasn't.

Tom bit back the sour taste of disappointment. It was ridiculous to feel this way. The men who saw her photo-graph would not know her name, where she lived, or the fact that she was married. They would see only a haunt-ingly beautiful woman, Tom's Fourth of July Woman. That was what was important, not the fact that Tom had this ridiculous feeling that someone had stolen something pre-cious from him. He'd been driving too long, searching for too many weeks. He was tired, and so he was overreacting.

"I'm sorry, Mrs. York." As he pronounced the words, Tom tried not to frown. This was getting to be absurd. He'd met the perfect woman, and all he did was apologize. Tak-ing photographs was his job, and he was good at it. He needed to remember that. He needed to focus on what was important—convincing the hauntingly beautiful Mrs. Mar-tha York to pose for him.

"My name is Tom Fleming," he continued, giving her

the smile that his mother claimed would charm the scales off a snake. Martha York was not a snake and she certainly had no scales, but Tom most definitely needed to charm her. "I'm a photographer with the *Gainey Gazette,*" he said, referring to the newspaper that was rivaling *The Saturday Evening Post* and *Life.*

If he hadn't been watching her carefully, he might have missed the way she flinched and her sudden pallor. It wasn't the reaction he'd expected. Most people were excited about meeting a photographer, particularly one from a paper as famous as the *Gainey Gazette.* But Mrs. Martha York, it appeared, was not most people. Her obvious hesitation—surely it hadn't been fear—only added to her allure.

When the color returned to her face, Tom continued. "I'd like to talk to you somewhere more private . . . perhaps outside." What he had to ask her was far too important to discuss here, with the shopkeeper hanging on his every word. "I saw a park across the street."

The shopkeeper regarded Tom with overt suspicion but directed his words to Martha York. "You be careful, Martha." Though Canela might claim to be the Friendliest Little Town in East Texas, this particular resident's primary characteristic appeared to be protectiveness. Perhaps the friendship was reserved for residents.

As a smile tilted Martha's lips upward, Tom took another deep breath. He had thought she was beautiful before, but when she smiled, she was truly breathtaking. He needed to capture that smile on a plate. Today, if possible.

"I don't imagine that Mr. Fleming intends any harm." Though Tom suspected she was amused by the shopkeeper's protectiveness, there was no hint of it in her voice. Instead, she spoke so calmly that Mr. Martin could not help but feel reassured.

"I assure you that I do not." All he wanted was to convince her to let him use her image. It would take a day, maybe two, to be sure that he had the perfect photograph. Then he'd be on his way back to New York. Sidney would be happy, and so would he. The Fourth of July Woman's picture would restore Tom Fleming's reputation as one of the country's preeminent photographers.

He opened the shop door and ushered Martha outside, then, careful to keep her on his right side, he offered her his arm as they crossed the street. "This is a pleasant park," he said, leading her to one of the benches nestled beneath an old oak tree. The light breeze that he'd felt when he had entered Canela had dissipated, making Tom thankful for the tree's shade.

Martha York's lips curved up again in what appeared to be amusement, but her voice was cool when she spoke. "Yes, it is pleasant, though I doubt you came to Canela to assess the beauty of our parks."

There was no point in skirting the issue. "I came looking for the perfect woman, and I found her—you."

The amusement faded abruptly, and those lovely turquoise eyes turned cold. "I don't understand the game you're playing, Mr. Fleming, but I assure you that I'm not perfect. Far from it."

There was rejection in her tone, and the way she shifted her weight forward told Tom she was close to bolting. He couldn't let that happen. He couldn't lose her. Martha York was the perfect Fourth of July Woman. Her picture was the one he needed to end the dry spell and salvage his career. Somehow he had to persuade her to let him photograph her. That was all it would take. Once she saw the pictures, she'd be convinced. "Perhaps you don't see yourself as others do." Tom made his voice as persuasive as he could.

"I have no illusions about myself." As she started to turn away, Tom leaned forward so that he could watch her lips. He didn't want to miss a single word. "I know who and what I am," she continued. "I'm Martha York, Canela's schoolteacher and a very ordinary woman."

A schoolteacher. That explained the patient tone when she'd spoken to the shopkeeper. Tom felt his spirits rise. She was probably a logical person. He'd appeal to that side of her. "Let me explain what I want. I've already told you that I'm a photographer. Independence Day is coming."

She raised one eyebrow to register her annoyance. "Believe it or not, Mr. Fleming, we have calendars in Canela, and I'm well aware of the national holiday."

She meant to rebuff him. Tom knew that. What he didn't understand was why. He could have sworn that she'd felt the same tug, the almost magnetic force, that had drawn him to her. It was more than ordinary attraction. It was a feeling of rightness, a conviction that he was meant to find her. "The *Gazette* is distributed to our men at the front lines," Tom said, hoping she'd listen and understand. "I wanted to have something special for them this year on Independence Day." Though it was so brief that he could have thought he imagined it, Tom knew that she had smiled when he'd said the word *special.* "I sold my editor on the idea of publishing a picture of someone I've been calling the Fourth of July Woman, and I've spent the last month searching for her."

Martha shifted on the bench, apparently uncomfortable with the direction the conversation was heading. Though it made no sense, Tom had the impression that she was battling fear. When she spoke, though, her voice was as calm as if she were addressing her pupils. "I'm confused, Mr. Fleming. Am I supposed to congratulate you on your persistence or commiserate with you that you've traveled so far?"

She wasn't going to agree. The sinking feeling in his stomach told Tom that this meeting was not going to end the way he wanted. He couldn't let that happen. He needed her. "Neither," he said. "And for Pete's sake, please don't call me Mr. Fleming. It makes me feel as old as my father. My name is Tom."

As Martha York shook her head slowly, her hair bounced against her cheeks. "It would hardly be seemly for me to address a casual acquaintance by his first name." The schoolteacher in her was stating a fact.

"I hope we'll be more than casual acquaintances." The most successful portraits were the ones where he had established a rapport with the subjects, when he understood what made them different from everyone else. Tom tried his charming smile again. "Don't you see? You're the woman I've been searching for. You're the perfect Fourth of July Woman." It was to no avail. She was not impressed. That was clear, for her expression remained skeptical. "I want to make you famous, Martha York."

The perfect Fourth of July Woman rose and prepared to leave. "I have no desire to be famous, Mr. Fleming, nor do I have any intention of being photographed," she said firmly. "A quiet life here in Canela is all I've ever wanted."

Tom couldn't let her go. "Think of what it would mean to the men," he said, hoping his voice did not reveal his desperation.

She shook her head again. "I'm sorry, Mr. Fleming, but the answer is no."

It was not the answer Tom wanted. It was not the answer he needed. He thought quickly. There had to be a way to persuade her. "Don't you want to be part of the war effort?"

This time she raised both eyebrows. "I've given my share to this war." Martha York started to walk away, then turned back. "What about you? If you care so much about the war, why aren't you fighting?"

Tom blinked, surprised by both the fierceness of her attack and the sense of inadequacy that he had never been able to shake.

"They wouldn't take me."

Martha rapped the egg against the rim, cringing when shards of shell fell into the bowl. Though ordinarily she enjoyed cooking and found it relaxing, today her thoughts were in such turmoil that she was having difficulty completing even the simplest of tasks.

How could she have been so rude? She, who had been raised to be polite to everyone, had behaved inexcusably. It was true that she had been flustered because of her reaction to him. From the moment she had turned around and seen Tom Fleming driving down Broad Street, she had felt as if something were drawing her to him. It reminded Martha of the experiments she had done with her pupils, showing them how a magnet attracted iron filings and how a flannel board attracted pictures with flannel backings. Those were simple, predictable reactions to physical properties, but there was nothing simple nor predictable about the way she had felt when she was near Tom Fleming.

Martha had been around dozens of men in her life. She had been in love, and she'd married the man she loved, but never had she felt like that. She could lie to herself and pretend that she'd been reacting to Tom's appearance. After all, the man was almost unfairly handsome. She could claim that her attraction had been physical, like the iron filings. But Martha was not one who lied to herself. What she had felt was more than physical. She had felt as if she and Tom were somehow connected, and that frightened her. Since she hadn't known how to fight the feeling, she had reacted instinctively and retreated behind a wall.

Martha picked up another egg and cracked it, taking care not to shatter the shell, then poured two tablespoons of milk into the bowl. It was a ridiculous idea, using her photograph in the *Gainey Gazette*. Even if she were willing to have her picture taken—which she was not—Martha's face wasn't one that inspired anyone. She knew that. Even Henry, who had loved her since they were children, hadn't told her she was beautiful, much less perfect. She wasn't either of those, and Tom Fleming had to be crazy if he thought otherwise. Martha frowned. Even if he was crazy and even if she hated the idea of giving anyone her photograph, that was no excuse for her asking him why he wasn't fighting. A well-bred lady didn't do things like that. A well-bred lady didn't pry into a stranger's life. But Martha had. And when she had heard his explanation, she had felt worse than she had in months.

Grabbing a fork, Martha began to beat the eggs. Perhaps scrambling them would help unscramble her thoughts. She should have recognized the signs, the way Tom kept her on his right side, even though at one point that had placed her next to the street, the way he watched her lips when she spoke. As a teacher, she should have realized that he was hard of hearing. She shouldn't have had to ask; she shouldn't have embarrassed him that way. For she had embarrassed Tom. Though it had been fleeting, he had been unable to hide the momentary pain Martha's question had caused. His eyes had darkened, and his lips had thinned.

When he spoke, his voice had been matter-of-fact, as if he were discussing nothing more important than yesterday's weather. He was totally deaf in his left ear, and the hearing in his right ear was impaired. That, he said, was why the Army had rejected him, why they wouldn't let him go to the war zone, even as a noncombatant. Though he had said nothing more, it was clear that he had wanted to join the Army and that the rejection still hurt. Poor Tom.

Martha gripped the fork handle as she blinked. When had she started thinking of him as Tom and not Mr. Fleming? How ridiculous. After all, she would never see him again.

It was probably a mistake. Tom laid his camera on the table, then looked at the room he had just agreed to rent. Though it was of average size, the table was an unexpected bonus. Once he had covered the window with a heavy blanket, he could develop and print his pictures on the table.

Assuming, that is, that there were any photographs to develop.

He should not have stayed. Time was running out, and he could not afford to waste a single day. Since Martha York had made it very clear that she did not want him to use her picture, he ought to have continued on to San Antonio and the West. Surely there was another woman in these United States and its territories who could be the Fourth of July Woman. Martha York couldn't be the only one whose face would inspire him.

If only it were that simple. Tom sighed as he emptied his valise onto the bed and sorted through the items. His first impression had been accurate. There was no reason to continue his search. Martha York would be the perfect Fourth of July Woman, and now that he'd seen her, he knew that no one else would satisfy him. There was no point in continuing his search. Tom had never settled for second best, and he had no intention of doing so now, not when so much hinged on one picture.

All he needed to do was convince her. He hadn't thought it would be difficult. When he had first studied photography, Tom's teachers had told him that people rarely refused to be photographed. No one had until today. No one had until Martha. She was the most unusual woman he'd ever met. Though she was cool on the surface, Tom sensed the warmth underneath, and that intrigued him as much as her refusal had.

Why wouldn't she let him photograph her? He doubted she would tell him, but perhaps someone in Canela would. That was one of the reasons Tom had sought a room with a family that offered meals as well as lodging. In his experience, gossip was frequently served along with the meat and potatoes.

"So, tell me, Tom," Hank Bradley said as he passed the bowl of pork and beans that were, since today was a meatless Tuesday, devoid of pork. "What brings a famous photographer like you to Canela?"

Tom looked at the man who sat at the head of the table. His new landlord was a tall, lean, middle-aged man, while his wife was short and plump. Was it true that opposites attracted? Was that why Tom found Martha York so interesting? She was certainly different from him. While travel was as vital to him as oxygen, she claimed that she had no desire to set foot outside the town limits. While he sought fame, she shunned it. And while he felt no need to encumber himself with permanent relationships, she had loved a man enough to marry him. Tom swallowed, unsure why that last thought was so painful. He wouldn't think about it. Instead, he'd learn what he could from the Bradleys.

"I'm traveling around the country, looking for scenes to photograph." That was true. If it wasn't the whole truth, well, the Bradleys didn't need to know everything. It was enough that they'd agreed to rent him their spare room and provide three meals a day. Tom owed them rent. He'd paid that willingly, but he had no intention of providing more gossip for a small town's rumor mill. He wanted to be the recipient of the rumors, not the grist that fed the mill.

"This is a mighty pretty town." Hank buttered a piece of cornbread.

"Indeed it is. That's why I thought I'd spend a few days here." Surely it wouldn't take more than a couple of days to wear down Martha York's resistance.

"The people are friendly." Linda Bradley smiled at Tom, as if to demonstrate that her hometown's slogan was fact, not fiction.

Nodding slowly, Tom said, "I met a couple of residents: Mr. Martin and a woman named Mrs. York." He spoke casually, as if he had no more interest in Martha than he did in the shopkeeper, but—if he had read Linda Bradley correctly—his landlady was a woman who liked to display her knowledge.

"Martha York's had a hard life these past few years," she said.

Her husband laid down his fork and frowned. "Now, Linda . . ."

She shook her head, unwilling to stop. "It's not a secret. Tom will hear the story sooner or later."

This was what he had hoped for. Trying to keep his enthusiasm hidden, Tom swallowed a bite of cornbread before he spoke. "You needn't say anything more if you're uncomfortable."

"Nonsense." Linda Bradley reacted the way he had hoped and launched into her tale with obvious relish. "Everyone knows that Martha Wentworth married Henry York; it'll be four years this June. She was the prettiest bride you ever did see." Tom didn't doubt that for a moment. "She had just turned twenty-two; in fact, they were married on her birthday." Linda's eyes misted the way women's frequently did when they spoke of weddings. For his part, Tom had never seen why the ladies got so teary-eyed over marriage. Weren't those supposed to be happy occasions?

A light breeze stirred the gingham curtains, and outside a dog barked. It was an ordinary day in an ordinary town. Tom suspected that the story was also an ordinary one. It was only the fact that it was Martha's story that gave it extra significance.

"It wasn't even a couple of months later when war broke out." Linda pursed her lips as if what she was going to say pained her. "We weren't in the war, of course, but that didn't stop Henry. He went off to Canada and enlisted with his cousins." The tone of her voice left no doubt that she did not approve of Henry York's actions. Tom's reaction was simpler. It wasn't a matter of approval or disapproval. In his case, it was a matter of disbelief. He couldn't understand why any man would willingly leave his bride if that bride was Martha. Linda Bradley frowned. "Henry was killed a few months later."

Martha was a widow. The realization hit Tom with a greater force than the knowledge that she was married. So much made sense now. The sorrow behind her cool facade hadn't been imaginary. It was real, and it had a very real cause. Martha wasn't saddened by the war in general. Her loss was personal. "That must have been difficult for Mrs. York." And Henry York must have been quite a man, for it was apparent that his widow's grief was still fresh, more than three years later.

Linda nodded. "Her parents had just died, so it was a bad spell for her. Luckily, the town hadn't been able to find a new schoolteacher and Martha had agreed to stay on until they hired a replacement. With Henry gone, there was no need to keep looking." Linda passed the bowl of beans, urging Tom to take another serving. "Then, too, Martha had her brother and sisters. She moved back into the family home to take care of them. That girl always was the most practical of the Wentworths." The last sentence was spoken so softly that Tom had to strain to hear her. Linda Bradley's Texas drawl was more pronounced than her husband's and she was seated to his left, which meant that Tom had to watch her lips carefully.

She continued speaking. "For the first couple years, things were fine. Then Theo—that's the Wentworth son— enlisted. A few months later Carolyn joined the nurses, and just last month Emily went over there." Though Linda did not say so, Tom assumed that Carolyn and Emily were Martha's sisters. "I reckon that big old house feels mighty lonely these days."

The beans, which had tasted delicious a few minutes ago, lost their flavor, and Tom swallowed with difficulty. He had wanted to learn about his Fourth of July Woman, and he had. What he hadn't reckoned with was his own reaction to what he'd learned. Something deep inside Tom ached as he realized that it was no wonder Martha had declared that she'd done her share for the war. The woman had lost everyone near to her, at least temporarily.

Tom took a long swallow of the cool tea that everyone in the South seemed to drink. He wasn't certain what surprised him more, the intense need he felt to comfort Martha or the knowledge that he'd never before felt this way. He'd been to Boston and Borneo and many places in between. He had spoken with royalty and ragged beggars. He'd experienced avalanches and earthquakes, the Aurora Borealis and a total eclipse. But never before had he met a woman like Martha York and never before had he felt like this.

There had to be a logical explanation. There was a logical explanation for everything, but for the life of him, Tom couldn't find it. And that worried him most of all.

Chapter Three

"Good morning."

Martha couldn't help it. She blinked in surprise, and then—though she tried to keep a telltale blush from coloring her face—felt warmth rise to her cheeks. This was silly. She was no longer sixteen years old. There was no reason to be embarrassed that a man was at her front gate and that he appeared to have been waiting for her. He stood outside the white picket fence, his posture as casual as if he did this every day of the week. Martha looked in both directions. The Model T was not in sight.

"Good morning, Mr. Fleming." She closed her front door and walked toward him, hoping that her rosy cheeks could be attributed to the early morning sunshine. It was one thing to tell herself she shouldn't be embarrassed. It was another to deny that she was curious. Martha shifted her books to her other arm. Why was Tom Fleming still in Canela? She had been certain that he would have left town last night. There was no reason for him to stay, particularly after the way she had treated him. But since he was still here, perhaps she could make amends.

"Call me Tom," he said, his lips curving into a smile that Martha suspected could charm an armadillo out of his plates. She was no armadillo, just a very ordinary woman, but the smile was certainly working on her. Though her mother would have frowned on it, insisting that relative strangers should not address each other so informally, Martha was actually considering using the man's first name.

As she approached the front gate, he opened it for her. It appeared that not only was Tom Fleming blessed with more than his share of physical beauty, but he also possessed impeccable manners.

"Good morning, Tom," Martha said. No thunderbolts split the sky. The earth did not crumble beneath her feet. Despite her mother's admonitions, it appeared that there were no terrible consequences from speaking Tom Fleming's name aloud. That was good. It also meant that there was no reason why she should not continue to speak to him. There was no question of etiquette involved in expressing regrets. "I want to apologize for my rudeness yesterday."

A speculative look appeared in his eyes. "Does that mean you've reconsidered being my Fourth of July Woman?"

From the corner of her eye, Martha saw her neighbor's curtains part. Though her face was not visible, Martha knew that Mrs. Bleeker was watching her and Tom. She shook her head. "It means I'm sorry that I pried into your private life." She stood next to him, staying on his right side and keeping her head turned toward him as she spoke. Now that she was aware of his hearing problem, Martha would do everything she could to minimize it.

"A man can try." Tom shrugged, as if her refusal was of little import. That surprised Martha, for yesterday she had sensed urgency in his request. Tom reached toward her. "Here, let me take those," he said, gesturing at her books. "I assume you're on your way to school."

The man was full of surprises. No one had carried her books in more years than Martha cared to count. It was true that Henry had done so when they were first courting, but

Tom was not Henry. He wasn't courting her; he was simply being polite.

"Your mother certainly taught you good manners," Martha said as she handed her books to Tom and started walking up the street.

He shrugged. "Mother used to say that a gentleman was welcome anywhere. At the time that she was teaching me the difference between salad and fish forks, I didn't see the value of her lessons, but I have to admit that etiquette has served me well on my travels."

"I imagine you've seen a lot of the country." After she had washed the supper dishes, Martha had dug through the pile of old *Gainey Gazettes* in her parlor, looking for Tom's pictures. What she had seen had impressed her, as had the fact that he was known as the Peripatetic Photographer. Apparently travel was as natural to Tom as taking beautiful pictures. Whether he photographed landscapes or people, each of his pictures had a special something that distinguished it from the others. Martha couldn't define what made them unique, other than to say that he appeared to view life differently from his colleagues.

A photographic study of the Grand Canyon that featured the work of three artists had pointed out the differences. One of the photographers had shown the Grand Canyon from the rim, focusing on the majesty of the gorge. Another had stood at the canyon's bottom next to the river and sighted the top. While his picture had been as beautiful as the first man's, it was Tom's photograph of a squirrel peering over the rim that had riveted Martha's attention. Perhaps it was the juxtaposition of the small animal and the immense canyon. Perhaps it was the contrast between the squirrel's soft fur and the harsh rock. Perhaps it was simply the addition of a living creature. Martha didn't know. All she knew was that when she closed her eyes, she felt as if that image were etched in her memory.

"Before the war, I traveled around the world." Tom

spoke the words as calmly as if he were announcing that he had walked to the other end of Main Street.

"Literally?" Martha had never known anyone who had even considered such a journey, much less actually taken it. Most of Canela's residents stayed close to home and considered a trip to the Gulf of Mexico a major undertaking. Henry had been different. For as long as Martha had known him, he had talked about visiting Europe. In her darker moments, she had wondered whether one of the reasons he had enlisted in the war was that it gave him the opportunity to realize his ambition.

"Literally." Tom's voice brought her back to reality. "What about you? Have you traveled much?"

As they crossed Broad Street, Martha waved to one of her neighbors. Perhaps alerted by Mrs. Bleeker, this woman stood on her front porch, ostensibly watering her potted plants but, Martha was willing to wager, actually keeping a watch out for her and Tom. When they reached the other side of the street, Martha shook her head in response to Tom's question. Travel was not something she enjoyed. "The only time I've been out of Texas was on my honeymoon. We went to Canada."

She tried not to frown. The one time she and Henry had argued had been over the destination of their honeymoon. Martha had wanted to go to Galveston, but Henry, whose family spent several weeks each summer with Canadian relatives, had insisted that he wanted to introduce his bride to the rest of his family.

"Canada is beautiful."

Martha couldn't argue with that. "I enjoyed Niagara Falls." That had been their first stop, before they visited Henry's cousins, and those two days had been the happiest of the fortnight. But her honeymoon wasn't something Martha wanted to recall. She would rather talk about something, almost anything, else. "What is the most beautiful place you've seen?" she asked. They had turned left on

Alamo Street and were close to the school now. If she kept Tom talking about his travels, perhaps she could avoid talking about, even thinking about, her own life.

He stared into the distance for a moment, as if considering. "It's difficult to say," he admitted at last. "If I had to choose, I'd say either Hawaii or Costa Brava." When Martha raised an eyebrow, silently telling Tom that she didn't know where Costa Brava was, he continued. "That's the Mediterranean coast of Spain between Barcelona and the French border. The words mean 'wild coast' in Spanish, and believe me, it's no exaggeration. The cliffs are breathtaking."

He sounded so enthusiastic that for a moment Martha found herself wishing she could see this wild coast. It was foolish, of course. The world was at war. No one traveled to Europe for pleasure. Besides, she didn't enjoy traveling. The trip to Canada had proven that.

"Canela must seem ordinary compared to the places you've seen." Martha gestured toward the buildings that lined Alamo Street. Everything in Canela was painted white, even the schoolhouse. While Martha agreed that the consistency avoided ugly clashes of color, there were times when she found the homogeneity boring. "There's nothing breathtaking here."

"You're here." His words were so unexpected that Martha stopped and stared at Tom. Though the words were ordinary, the way he was looking at her could never be described as ordinary. His gaze wasn't clinical. Martha didn't feel as if she were being studied. Instead, she felt as if she were being . . . appreciated. It was an unusual feeling and one that made her pulse begin to race at the same time that another blush stained her cheeks.

"You're embarrassing me."

"I didn't mean to." When Tom met her gaze, his expression seemed sincere. "I simply wish I could convince you to pose for me."

He was persistent. There was no denying that. Most people would have given up after the way she'd refused them, unless something important was at stake. Since Martha doubted that any one picture was critical to Tom's survival as a photographer, she discounted that reason. There had to be another. As they approached the schoolhouse, Martha stopped and stared at Tom for a moment. He reminded her of Sally Jenkins and Emil Morgan. Perhaps that was the reason for his persistence. "Are you an only child?"

The question obviously took Tom by surprise, for his eyes widened a fraction. "Yes, I am, but why did you ask?"

Pleased to have her hypothesis confirmed, Martha nodded. "I thought so. You remind me of several of my students who have no siblings. They're not used to having anyone say no to them."

As Tom stared in amazement, Martha reclaimed her books and climbed the stairs to the schoolhouse.

Could she be right? For a moment after Martha disappeared into the schoolhouse, Tom stood there, staring at the whitewashed building. If it weren't for the fact that it was white rather than the more traditional red, Canela's school looked like dozens of others that Tom had seen, several of which he had photographed. The square building had a single window on each side, a door at the front, and an unbroken wall at the back. Even without entering the room, Tom knew that the back wall held the chalkboard, just as he knew that in a few minutes someone would ring the bell. What he didn't know was why Martha's words bothered him.

He took a step forward, planning to go inside and ask her why she did not find persistence to be a virtue. Then, as a gaggle of giggling girls approached, Tom turned and walked rapidly in the opposite direction. A man needed to know when to make a strategic retreat. It was one thing to provoke the adults' gossip in a small town, quite another

to face the relentless questioning of the younger generation.
Tom had done that twice and had no intention of repeating
the experience. Though they didn't mean to, children could
be as annoying as a horde of Alaskan mosquitoes.

He turned left on Elm, heading back toward the center
of town. Was Martha's diagnosis accurate? It was discon-
certing to think that he could be so easily characterized and
yet Tom suspected there was more than a little truth to her
accusation. *No* was not a word he had heard frequently as
a child. In fact, as he thought about it, his parents had
denied him nothing. Tom had merely to express a want,
and it was fulfilled. When he was old enough to realize that
not all children were so fortunate, he had thought that the
reason his parents indulged him was his deafness. Now
Tom wondered if that had been the only reason. Perhaps
Martha was right, and his parents had doted on him because
they had no one else on whom to lavish attention.

Tom paused when he reached Broad Street. If he turned
left, he'd pass the stores he'd seen yesterday as he had
entered Canela. If he continued on Elm, he'd see nothing
but houses. The sight of schoolchildren on Broad made the
decision. Tom continued east on Elm.

She was an unusual woman, this Martha York. She was
perceptive. Though he had a healthy regard for women's
intuition, Tom knew that not all women were as perceptive
as Martha. That alone would have intrigued him. But there
was more to Martha than a heightened sense of intuition.
The canopy of trees was sparser here, the shade sun dap-
pled. As his eyes tried to adjust to a particularly bright
patch, Tom realized that the shade reminded him of Martha.
Like it, she was an intriguing blend of contrasts, cheerful
at one moment, but obviously harboring deep sorrows.
Though she had tried to mask it, Martha had been unable
to hide her sadness when she spoke of her honeymoon.

Tom frowned, not liking the direction his thoughts had
taken. For Pete's sake, he was a photographer, not a poet.

Why was something as ordinary as sun-dappled shade making him think about Martha York? And why were those thoughts so disturbing?

Tom gritted his teeth. He had heard about love that defied death. The ancient Greeks had glorified such love, and the modern poets had waxed eloquent over it. Tom knew about it in theory, but never before had he seen it. He ought to be in awe of such a powerful emotion. Instead, he found himself facing an unexpected reaction. There was no point in denying it. Tom Fleming was envious. Though he had accomplished many things in his life, he had never inspired a love like that. That bothered him. What was worse was the feeling that, even if he were to live to be a hundred, he would never be loved the way Henry York was.

He wouldn't think about that. There was nothing he could do to change it. What was important was convincing Martha York to pose for a photograph. Once Tom had captured her likeness on film, he could return to New York, and his life would be back in equilibrium. He would have his Fourth of July Woman. Sidney would be happy enough to give Tom a new assignment. Why stop at that? Sidney would be so pleased with the pictures that he would give Tom all the choice assignments. The other photographers would envy Tom the way he envied Henry York.

He wouldn't think about that man. Tom spun around on his heel and headed back into town. School didn't end until the afternoon. Until then, he had nothing to do other than think of arguments that might succeed where his earlier ones had failed. He would convince Martha. He had to.

Tom turned onto Main Street. He might as well see what the center of town had to offer. Surely there was more than he had seen last night. He walked slowly, looking at each of the stores' plate-glass windows. And with each one, Tom's puzzlement grew. What was it that Martha found so attractive about her hometown? Oh, he could see that a person might find it restful. The lack of traffic might be a pleasant contrast to teeming city streets for a day or two. But after that, life in Canela would undoubtedly prove to be boring. As far as Tom could see, there was little to do. He had seen a small library, and there was a movie theater on the same block as the park, but surely there should be more. What did people do besides gossip?

Tom pulled out his watch. Three more hours until Linda Bradley had said she was serving the noon meal. What on earth was he going to do for three hours in the most boring town in East Texas? Though he needed nothing, Tom opened the door to the general store. Perhaps he could while away a few minutes here.

"Good morning." Mr. Martin greeted him with such enthusiasm that Tom guessed the man was as bored as he'd been. "I heard you're staying with Hank and Linda Bradley."

"News travels fast here." According to the Bradleys, almost everyone in town was on the telephone line. That must help in transmitting gossip.

"I reckon it does." The shopkeeper leaned on the counter. "Everyone's trying to figger out why you're here." His expression changed to one that Tom could only describe as conspiratorial, and he lowered his voice, though there was no one else in the store. "Hank says you're taking pictures, but I figger that's just a cover-up."

A cover-up. Tom wasn't certain which he found more amusing, the man's expression or the thought that he might be involved in a clandestine activity. "What made you think that?" he asked.

The man nodded sagely. "Others might not have figgered it out, but I can put two and two together."

It was Tom's turn to nod. Perhaps the morning wasn't going to be as boring as he'd feared. Perhaps this was the town's entertainment: listening to Mr. Martin's tales. For Tom suspected that when the shopkeeper put two and two together, the result would be more than four.

"I knew it was a cover-up when you asked to talk to Martha in private." Tom simply nodded, encouraging the man to continue. This was definitely more interesting than walking down Main Street, peering into shop windows. "I figger the Army sent you."

The Army. Now Tom was part of a clandestine activity involving the military. Interesting. He nodded again.

"There's only one reason I figger anyone from the Army wants to talk to Martha, and that's her brother."

"Theo?"

A delighted grin crossed Mr. Martin's face. "I knew it. I never did believe that story that he was killed. I always figgered a boy as smart as Theo wouldn't get himself killed."

Tom's stomach knotted in pain, and the amusement that the shopkeeper's story had generated vanished. Killed. How had Linda Bradley missed telling him that part of the story? She had been quick to say that Martha's husband had died in the war, but she had not mentioned her brother. Poor Martha! No wonder she said she had done her share for this awful war.

Tom thought rapidly. He'd seen one blue and one gold star in Martha's front window. The gold was undoubtedly for Henry. Did the fact that the other was still blue mean that Martha shared Mr. Martin's doubts?

He gave the shopkeeper an appraising look. "I wish I could tell you that you were right." There was no exaggeration in Tom's statement. He did indeed wish he could confirm that Martha's brother was still alive. If he could, perhaps some of the sorrow that seemed to cling to her like moss to the trees in the Olympic Peninsula would dissipate.

The shopkeeper nodded again. "I reckon it's still class-y-fied. You don't need to worry, Mr. Fleming. I know how to keep a secret. I'm not like some folks here in town."

Two minutes earlier, Tom would have found the garrulous Mr. Martin's assertion that he was discreet humorous.

But now nothing seemed funny. Now he wondered how one woman could endure so much tragedy.

"For a woman who doesn't like being the center of attention, you certainly have gotten the town talking about you." A smile creased Anna's round face as she turned from the window and greeted Martha. "Three different people telephoned me last night to tell me you and a stranger had been seen sitting in the park. According to them, he was more handsome than John Barrymore. Naturally, I didn't believe them. But now . . ." Anna glanced back at the window, as if hoping to catch another glimpse of Tom Fleming. "Now he walks to school with you. Heavenly days! Canela will never be the same."

Martha tried not to laugh at Anna's dramatics. Although her friend was normally placid, when something piqued her interest, she could be as unpredictable as a hurricane. "I'd be happy to introduce you to him, but I doubt I'll see him again." Unless, of course, he still refused to admit that Martha would not change her mind. Surely the man was not so foolish as to entertain hopes of turning her into the Fourth of July Woman. She had been as clear with her refusal as she could without being rude.

Martha walked to the front of the room and laid her books on the desk. It was only in her imagination that the faint scent of Tom's soap clung to the binding. She needed to dismiss that notion just as she needed to ignore those thoughts of Tom that seemed to creep into her mind. She was Martha York, Canela's sensible schoolteacher, not a flighty young girl, dreaming about a handsome stranger.

"If I were ten years younger," Anna announced, "I wouldn't wait for an introduction. I'd be outside right now, finding a reason to talk to him. Alas," she said with a prolonged sigh, "I'm too old for him." Anna gave Martha an appraising look. "So, why is he here and why did he want to speak to you?"

It wasn't going to be easy dismissing thoughts of Tom when he was the only subject Anna wanted to discuss. "Your informants probably told you that he's a photographer." Anna nodded. "He wants to take pictures of me."

Martha's assistant clapped her hands. "*Wunderbar!*" It was a measure of Anna's excitement that she lapsed into her native German. Normally, although she still spoke with a light accent, her English was faultless.

"I refused."

"Why on earth did you do a foolish thing like that?" Anna demanded, her hands fisted on her hips, her expression almost comic.

Martha began to write the day's first assignment on the chalkboard. She had walked more slowly than normal today, which meant she would have to hurry to finish the lessons before the students arrived. "I don't want my picture in the *Gainey Gazette*," she told Anna. *Or anywhere,* she added silently.

"Surely you don't believe that old tale that if someone has your photograph, they have a part of you."

"Of course not." Martha was quick to reassure her friend. Though she recognized that her fears might not make sense to anyone else, that particular superstition was not the reason she had refused to be the Fourth of July Woman. Martha seized a convenient excuse. "You said it yourself: I don't want to be the center of attention." There was no reason to tell Anna that that was not the only reason Martha didn't want her photograph put on public display. Since her sisters had left Canela, Anna was Martha's closest friend, but there were things that even close friends did not need to know.

Fortunately, before Anna could continue her inquisition, the pupils began to arrive. From the moment that the first one entered the schoolhouse, it was evident that today would not be an ordinary day. The children bristled with excitement.

"Teacher," May Gibson cried, "we heard there's a famous man in town."

"Mama says he takes pictures," Paul Anderson chimed in. "Fancy ones."

Helen Sempert had no intention of being left out of the discussion. "My Pa says he's been everywhere. He said he was perry . . . perry . . . perry-something."

"Peripatetic." Martha pronounced the word carefully so that even the youngest could repeat it. "It means he travels a lot."

"Ooh. That's exciting."

Martha nodded as she helped the smallest children put their caps on the rack. She had long since learned that the easiest way to deal with the youngsters' enthusiasm was to let it run its natural course. But when they were seated and Martha walked to the front of the classroom, May raised her hand. "Can he come talk to us?"

"Yes, please!" The other students echoed the plea.

For a second, Martha was tempted to refuse. Tom Fleming was attractive and charming and far too disruptive to her equilibrium. It would be foolish to do anything that put her in more contact with him. But as she looked at the children's eager faces, Martha found herself nodding. Many of the students' fathers were gone, and though their mothers tried their best, Martha knew that the children had few sources of pleasure. "If he's still here this afternoon, I'll ask him," she agreed.

The cheer that greeted her words was more enthusiastic than the one that had accompanied yesterday's early dismissal.

When the last of the students left, Martha gathered her books. He wouldn't be there. There was no reason for him to be there. But as she looked out the window, she saw him standing across the street. Though his posture was casual, there was no denying the fact that Tom was watching the school.

"Anna, I think you're going to be able to meet the famous Mr. Fleming." The woman's Cheshire-cat grin told Martha she wasn't surprised. As the two women descended the stairs, Tom approached them. Martha performed the introductions, then watched, amused, as Tom proceeded to charm her assistant. It was with obvious reluctance that Anna turned toward her home.

"May I walk you home?" Tom asked when Anna was out of earshot.

Martha nodded. "We've provided a month's supply of grist for the rumor mill. What's a bit more?"

"Don't sound so gracious," he said, his smile defusing the seriousness of his words. "I thought you might enjoy my company."

"I'm sorry." The truth was, she did enjoy Tom's company, and there was certainly no harm in walking a few blocks with him. After all, the man would only be in town for another day or two. "It's simply that I'm not used to being Canela's primary topic of conversation."

Tom reached for her books and tucked them under his left arm, keeping her on his right side as they walked the half block to Oak Street. Martha had a routine. Each morning she would walk up Chestnut, turning left when she reached Alamo. In the afternoon, she would take Oak to Second and follow it to Chestnut, completing the circuit. It was only yesterday that she had varied her route, turning onto Broad. If she hadn't done that, she might not have met Tom. If she hadn't done that, she wouldn't have dreamt of a handsome blond stranger last night. If she hadn't done that, she wouldn't have had a room of squirming students today. How much of life, Martha wondered, depended on chance?

"From what I've heard, you do a lot for this town. Everywhere I go, I hear people talking about you." The way Tom smiled made Martha wonder who had provided the information. "I learned that not only do you teach, but you also arrange flowers for every occasion, and now you're even planning the Independence Day celebration."

Martha frowned. "I'm not doing too well with the last one," she admitted. "I wanted to find something to replace the fireworks, but my well of inspiration has run dry." That was one of the reasons she hoped Tom would agree to speak to the children. Though it would not compensate fully for the absence of fireworks, it would give them a happy memory.

Tom was silent for a moment, and the furrows she saw between his eyes told Martha he was thinking about her dilemma. "What about a kissing booth?" he suggested. Though his voice was solemn, those blue eyes that were as bright as an August sky sparkled.

One of the blushes that had become so common since Tom Fleming drove his Model T into Canela stained Martha's cheeks. "A kissing booth for the children?" What an outrageous thought!

"I suppose it wouldn't be appropriate for the youngest ones."

The man was impossible. "I don't know where you were raised, but in Canela children don't kiss."

The smile he gave her said Tom didn't believe a word of her protest. "For the record, I was raised in Rochester, New York. It may be farther north, but I suspect children are the same everywhere." He grinned. "I remember trying to kiss Victoria Chambers and getting my face slapped for it." The tone of his voice said the kiss was worth the slap.

She couldn't encourage him. She wouldn't encourage him. "I don't want any of my pupils being either slapped or kissed."

"All right," he agreed, his eyes still bright with mirth. "Let's think of something else. I would suggest a circus, but I doubt there's enough time to arrange for one."

"Time is the least of the worries. We don't have enough money. We've all bought so many Liberty Bonds that I'm afraid our budgets are very limited."

"I understand limited budgets." The furrows between Tom's eyes reappeared, and though he greeted Mrs. Fisher with as much courtesy as he'd displayed to the three other matrons who just happened to be sitting on their front porches as Tom and Martha walked by, she sensed that he was still considering her question. "What about a carousel?" he asked as they crossed First Street. "Have you ever had a merry-go-round here?"

Martha shook her head. Her only acquaintance with what many called painted ponies was through pictures. "I have to admit I've never even seen one."

"Never?" Tom's surprise was palpable. "We need to change that. Children love carousels, and so do adults."

"But wouldn't it be expensive?" Though Martha knew that there were traveling merry-go-rounds just as there were traveling circuses, she doubted Canela could afford one.

Tom shook his head. "Not if I asked Frank Patton to help you. I took photographs of one of his carousels, and that got him so much new business that he promised to loan one of his merry-go-rounds to any city I picked, free of charge. The truth is, I got a letter from Frank before I left New York, asking me if I'd found the town." Tom must have sensed her hesitation, for he continued. "If you're wondering why he'd make an offer like that, it's because Frank's a shrewd businessman. He knows that the free advertising will benefit him. As for me, I'd like to help solve your problem."

It was a generous offer. Martha knew that the children—not to mention the adults—would enjoy the carousel and that having it in Canela would more than compensate for the lack of fireworks. The question was, what would Tom expect in return? He was the most persistent man she'd ever met, and for reasons that were not clear to her, she was the object of his persistence. Was this part of his campaign to get her to agree that he could take her photograph?

"I'm not sure," Martha said, unwilling to put the reasons for her hesitation into words.

"There are no strings attached. I won't insist that you pose for me."

Martha nodded slowly, realizing that she had misjudged him. "I'll have to ask the rest of the committee," she said, "but I think I know their answer." They'd be fools to turn down an opportunity to provide the town with such a unique experience, and no one on the Independence Day committee was a fool. "Thank you, Tom."

As they walked along Chestnut Street toward Martha's house, she felt her uneasiness grow. In just a few minutes, Tom had solved the problem that had been plaguing her. Not only had he provided an idea for the July Fourth celebration, but he was offering her the solution itself at no cost to the town. Faced with that generosity, how could she ask him for another favor, even a minor one?

"Did I say something wrong?"

Martha blinked in surprise as she turned toward him. "No, not at all. Why did you ask?"

"You've been unusually quiet for the last block."

"I'm wrestling with a dilemma."

He raised an eyebrow. "Would I be out of turn if I asked if I were part of that dilemma?"

Martha shook her head. They had reached her front gate. In a minute she would climb the steps to her house, and Tom would return to the Bradleys'. If she didn't ask him now, she would be reneging on her promise to the children. "Your assumption is correct," she said. "The fact is, I have a favor to ask, and I'm feeling more than a little embarrassed about it. If it weren't for the children . . ."

Tom shrugged. "So just ask. What's the worst I can say?"

Martha thought back to her refusal of the night before. "You could say no."

"But you won't know whether or not I'll refuse until you ask."

"That's true." She took a deep breath, then let it out. "The children—my pupils—are very excited about having a famous person in town. You were all they wanted to talk about today." Martha started to pause, then forced herself to continue. "I wondered if you'd come to the school and speak to the children for a few minutes. It would mean a lot to them."

Tom was silent for so long that Martha wondered whether he was shocked by her request. At length he spoke. "What about you? Would it mean a lot to you too?"

Martha nodded. There was no point in denying it. "I'd be very grateful if you'd come."

"Grateful enough to let me take your photograph?"

It was what Martha had expected. "I'm not your Fourth of July Woman." She would do many, many things for the town of Canela and her pupils in particular, but she would not let her photograph be put in a national paper. Her fears might be irrational—most fears were—but she wouldn't take the risk. Though Martha hated to disappoint the children, this was one bargain she would not make.

She reached for the books that Tom was still holding, but he refused to return them to her. Instead, he gave her a long appraising look, as if he were trying to see behind her words. "Can we compromise?" he asked. "If you let me take the pictures, I promise I won't use them without your permission."

Martha wasn't sure what he hoped to accomplish, for she would never give her permission. Still, posing for a few photographs that would not be used was a small price to pay. There was no harm in having the pictures taken. The danger was only in how they were used. "If I agree, will you talk to the children?"

He nodded. "I'll come on Friday after I take the first photographs." It was clear he wasn't taking any chances that she'd renege.

"Do you really think that seeing them will make me change my mind?"

Tom's hair fell onto his forehead as he nodded again. "I'm counting on that, just as you're counting on me to come to the school."

"You drive a hard bargain, Tom Fleming."

He shrugged and brushed his hair back. "I like to win." That was what Martha feared. The problem was, his idea of winning wasn't the same as hers. "Do we have an agreement?"

It was her turn to nod.

"Shall we shake on it?"

Slowly, Martha extended her hand, placing it in his. It was a handshake, nothing more. This wasn't the first time she had shaken hands with a man; it certainly would not be the last. But when Tom's fingers touched hers, Martha knew that never before had a man's touch felt like this. Tom's hand was larger than hers, his grip firmer. The warmth of his hand was oddly comforting, sending shivers of pleasure up her arm, making her feel cherished, making her feel special, making her wish he would never, ever let go. Not even Henry's kisses had made her feel like this.

What on earth was happening to her?

Chapter Four

Everything was perfect: the lighting, the setting, and especially the woman. Today she was wearing a dark-blue dress that complimented her silver-blond hair. With the afternoon sun providing back lighting and the white picket fence in the foreground, it was the perfect setting for the perfect woman. Though she might deny it, Martha York was his Fourth of July Woman. Tom could hardly believe that she stood next to him, her hand clasped in his, her smile almost ethereal in its beauty.

"I wish I could take a picture of you looking like that."

She tugged her hand free from his, as if she had suddenly realized how long he had been holding it, and he felt a momentary sense of loss. If he'd had his way, Tom would have held her hand forever. "Like what?" she asked.

"Surprised, curious, and eager to learn, all at the same time." Her face had changed when she'd put her hand in his. A second earlier, she had been beautiful, but when they'd touched, her face had become radiant, as if something about the contact had electrified her. That meant that she had felt it, too. He hadn't been the only one who'd noticed that what was supposed to be a simple handshake had been something much more complex, something decidedly more exciting than a handshake had any right to be.

A sudden thought assailed Tom. Did his face reflect the same wonder? Did he have that starry-eyed look? Surely not. It was only a handshake, for Pete's sake. Besides, Tom was well schooled in camouflaging his thoughts. Of course Martha hadn't seen any difference in him. It was only because he was trained to watch people's expressions that he'd noticed the way her face had softened and brightened.

"I wish I had my camera," he said. It wasn't simply that he needed the photograph. That was important, of course, but the camera would have served another purpose. Staring into the focusing hood would help keep his mind off that all too disturbing feeling that holding Martha's hand had created.

"Why don't you have it with you?"

Why didn't he? Normally Tom would have carried the Graflex with him as he'd walked through town, but he hadn't wanted to alarm her.

"I wasn't sure you'd agree."

"And now that I have, you don't want to waste any time."

Tom nodded. "I'd like to take a few plates and develop them tomorrow. Where do folks in Canela have film processed?"

Although many press photographers had stopped doing their own developing and printing, instead shipping the exposed plates to their editors, Tom was unwilling to risk losing his negatives. He carried equipment and chemicals with him, preferring to be self-reliant rather than lose an irreplaceable photograph as he had when he had shipped undeveloped film back from Persia. But, depending on how long he stayed in Canela, he might need a new supply of developer and fixer.

"They mail the film back to Kodak." Martha's response told Tom he would need to find a source outside Canela.

"Ever since Mr. Harris died, we haven't had a real photographer in town."

"That explains why people are so curious about me."

Martha laughed as she shook her head, and once again Tom wished he had the Graflex and an unexposed plate. "No, it doesn't explain it. All Mr. Harris did was take portraits of people. Even at his best, he was mediocre. The reason everyone's excited about having you in Canela is that you're one of the finest photographers in the country. You're a celebrity."

Tom didn't feel like a celebrity. What he felt like was a man whose editor had lost confidence in him, a man who was no longer certain he could take pictures that were any better than the ones that Martha described as mediocre.

"I'd like to take some photographs today," he told her. The only way to prove that Sidney was wrong was to produce pictures that were as good as—no, better than—any he'd done before. With Martha as a subject, Tom knew he had an excellent chance of doing exactly that. The excitement that he'd felt when he'd seen her next to the fence held the same sense of anticipation, the same conviction that the photograph would be good that had always accompanied his very best shots.

"Wait right here," he said. "It will take me a few minutes to get my camera."

And, if luck was with him, one of the pictures he took today would be the one that would restore his reputation.

Martha stared at her reflection in the mirror as she brushed her hair. It was fortunate that photographers were not painters and worked only in black and white. At least that way, her blush would not be evident to anyone other than Tom. She couldn't explain it. She had never been a person who blushed easily, but since Tom Fleming had arrived in Canela, her face had felt as if it were permanently stained red. How ridiculous! It was just as ridiculous as the way she had felt when her hand had touched his.

Martha opened the door to her armoire, then shook her head. She would not change her clothing. Why should she when she had no intention of allowing Tom to use the photograph? Before she could change her mind, she descended the stairs and went outside.

She took a seat on the porch swing, hoping the slow motion would soothe her thoughts. Perhaps the cool air and the gentle rhythm of the swing would make that unfortunate blush disappear. It wasn't that she was embarrassed when she was with Tom. It was . . . What was it? Though she was a woman who taught children to read and who had a reasonably large vocabulary, Martha found herself unable to complete the sentence. She could not explain what it was about Tom that made her blush, just as she could not explain why something as simple as a handshake should have disturbed her the way it had.

The sound of an approaching automobile brought Martha's thoughts back to the present. Tom was indeed in a hurry if he had chosen to drive the short distance from the Bradleys' house to hers. With gasoline prices rising, hardly anyone in Canela drove if their destination was within the town limits.

"I hope you don't mind," Tom said as he opened the door and helped her into the passenger's seat, "but I thought I might use the car as part of the background. It's the all-American car, and you're the all-American woman."

Once again, color flooded Martha's face. "Do you do it deliberately?" she demanded. "Do you try to make me blush?" The lot across the street was empty, a fact that Martha and her siblings had appreciated as children, since it gave them a ready-made playground. Today Martha was grateful for the absence of a house, since it meant that she had no neighbors there to watch her and Tom. Mrs.

Bleeker, she knew, was at her quilting circle this afternoon, leaving only Tom to witness Martha's discomfort.

"Of course I'm not trying to embarrass you." Tom's voice sounded sincere. "Although I must admit that the extra color in your cheeks is very attractive."

She hadn't thought it possible, but Martha could feel her face redden even more. This couldn't continue. She couldn't continue to look like a ripe tomato. There had to be something she could do to get her wayward emotions under control. As Tom pulled his camera from the back seat, Martha focused her attention on it. Perhaps that would help her cool her face.

"What kind of camera is it?" she asked. "It's smaller than I expected." The camera Mr. Harris had used had been so large that it had required a sturdy tripod. Tom was holding this one in his hand.

"It's called a Graflex," he said. He released a catch on the top, causing a funnel-shaped piece to emerge. "Did Mr. Harris have a large black cloth that covered him and the back of the camera?" When Martha nodded, Tom pointed to the funnel. "This is called a focusing hood. It takes the place of the cloth." Tom looked into the focusing hood, then turned a button on the right side of the camera.

"You're a beautiful woman, Martha. Hasn't anyone told you that?"

Beautiful wasn't a word she had heard very often, at least not applied to her. Carolyn was the beautiful Wentworth sister, Emily the talented one. Martha was simply the practical Wentworth. Even when they'd been courting, Henry had not said she was beautiful. It was only her father who had called her his beautiful princess. "Not recently," she admitted.

Tom raised his head from the focusing hood, his expression clearly chagrined. "I'm sorry," he said. "I didn't mean to remind you of unhappy times."

Had he guessed that she had been thinking of Henry and

her father and how much she missed them? "These are all unhappy times."

Tom continued fiddling with his camera. Something he was doing was making the lens move in and out. "There's no denying that the war has changed most of our lives. The way I see it, that's all the more reason to find happiness wherever we can."

"Is this conversation part of another attempt to convince me that I should let you use my photograph?"

Tom looked up again. "Was I that obvious?"

"You're the most tenacious man I've ever met." Martha smiled as she realized that talking about Tom's persistence had made her blush disappear. "I need to warn you, though, that I'm stubborn, too."

"I never would have guessed."

His voice was so droll that Martha couldn't help it. She laughed.

"Perfect!" The camera clicked.

"You're sneaky!" She had been so busy concentrating on what Tom was saying that she hadn't realized he was ready to take a picture.

"I prefer the word 'tenacious.' Now, let me try another pose." Tom climbed out of the car and moved to the passenger's side. "Tip your face to the left," he said. "Like this." He stretched out his hand and touched her cheek, moving her head ever so slightly to the left.

It was worse than the handshake. Though the afternoon was cool, Martha's face was not. This time, the touch of his fingers made her cheeks flame and sent shivers running down her spine. She swallowed, trying to regain her composure. What was it about this man that even the lightest, most impersonal touch made her feel as if she'd been hit by lightning? It wasn't an unpleasant sensation, but it was disturbing.

Martha had always been known as the most sensible of the Wentworth sisters. She was the one who could be relied on to remain calm even in the face of traumatic events like her parents' and Henry's deaths. And now . . . now something as ordinary as a photographer helping her pose had caused an extraordinary reaction. Of course, Martha reflected, there was nothing ordinary about Tom Fleming. He was both an extraordinary photographer and an extraordinarily handsome man. The combination was enough to disturb anyone's equilibrium. That was it. That was why she was reacting the way she had. Martha smiled, relieved by the logical explanation.

The camera clicked again. "Good," Tom said as he returned to the driver's seat and started the car. "I'm not sure where I'll take the next pictures, so I thought we'd just drive through town."

Martha nodded as she settled back in the seat. Though the sight of her with Tom would undoubtedly precipitate a spate of telephone calls and back fence discussions, she had made a pact, and she would do her part.

"What do people in Canela do for entertainment?" Tom asked as they drove slowly along Forest Avenue. The street paralleled Chestnut but was less developed. Like most towns, Canela had begun as a two-road village with Main running east-west and Broad as the north-south route. As the population expanded, new streets were added, each one perfectly straight and parallel to either Main or Broad. Forest marked the northern boundary of the town. If Tom was looking for entertainment, he would not find it here.

"Entertainment besides gossip?" Martha raised an eyebrow.

As she had hoped, Tom grinned. "You mean there is something else?"

"Oh, yes." Martha held out a hand and began to count on her fingers. "Besides the movies, we have an amateur theater group. I doubt they can compare to Mr. Ziegfield's Follies or the other Broadway productions, but everyone enjoys the plays." She folded down a second finger. "Then there are the schoolchildren. There's not an empty seat when we present the Christmas pageant or the spring play." Another finger turned in toward her palm. "The churches have socials." Yet another finger. "The country club has dances, and I mustn't forget the parades." Her hand was now folded into a fist.

Martha looked at Tom, trying to gauge his reaction. He had been watching the street while he drove. Unlike Emily and Theo, who spent as much time looking out the side of the car as through the windscreen, Tom appeared to be concentrating on his driving. Martha wondered whether it was because of his hearing. Did he find that he needed to be especially alert? "It probably sounds dull to you."

Though he shook his head slightly, Martha couldn't tell whether or not Tom was disagreeing with her. "They're not things I've ever done," he admitted. Of course not. This was the man who had traveled around the world, the man who worked for a famous newspaper. "But," he said, "you make them sound like fun."

There was no hint of condescension in his voice. Martha smiled with pleasure. It seemed that Tom understood. "Life in Canela isn't necessarily exciting, but it is fun, or at least it was before the war. We have such wonderful people that I wouldn't want to live anywhere else."

As he turned the car left on Brazos, Tom looked skeptical. "Surely you want to travel."

Martha pursed her lips. Tom was right about many things, but this was one area where he was wrong. "The rest of my family has done that. Canela is good enough for me."

His head swiveled, his eyes leaving the road as he gave her a long look, his expression saying he was startled by her vehemence. "Then will you be my guide for a few days? I'd like you to show me your town."

Martha blinked, as surprised by his request as he'd been by her refusal to travel. She had thought he'd leave as soon as he had spoken to the schoolchildren on Friday. Surely by then he would realize that she was not going to allow him to use her photograph. Perhaps he was staying in the hope of convincing her. She wouldn't change her mind. She knew that, and by now Tom ought to, as well. Still, if he wanted to stay . . . It was foolish, but the prospect of seeing Tom again warmed Martha as much as his compliments had.

"I heard you and Martha York were out driving together today." Hank Bradley leaned back in the porch rocker and tapped his pipe. They had finished dinner, and while Linda washed the dishes, Hank had invited Tom to join him on the porch.

Tom tried not to sigh as he settled in the other chair. He should have realized that the news of his brief automotive excursion would travel considerably faster than the Model T had. "She's agreed to be my guide to Canela," he said as evenly as he could. He had decided that he would take pictures of the town, hoping they would serve two purposes. If she saw him photographing other things, perhaps Martha would be more relaxed in front of the camera. And if the townspeople learned that he was taking pictures of their landmarks, perhaps they would not realize that Martha was the only reason he was in Canela. They would know when the *Gainey Gazette* published the picture of the Fourth of July Woman, for Tom was confident that Martha would agree to let him use it once she had seen her photograph, but there was no need to subject her to additional speculation until then.

"She's a good woman."

Tom wouldn't argue with that. "She seems to know a great deal about the town." And she was definitely the most beautiful woman in Canela, although he saw no reason to share that opinion with Hank Bradley. He also wouldn't tell Hank that her face was almost as smooth as the silks he'd purchased in India or that his fingertips had tingled when they'd touched her cheeks.

"I reckon that's why she's a schoolteacher," the older man said, " 'cause she knows so much." He struck a match and lit his pipe. "I always did like Martha the best of the Wentworth children. There's no nonsense about her."

"Indeed." Tom wished he could make her laugh more often, but that might not be possible. The woman had lost so much. Perhaps she had also lost the ability to laugh freely.

"The only thing I don't understand is why she lets that German work at the school." Though the sun had set, enough light spilled through the kitchen window that Tom could see Hank scowl as he bit his pipe stem.

"Anna Gottlieb?"

"Yep." Hank puffed on his pipe. "If you ask me, the government should have sent all those Germans back to their country when the war began. It's plumb foolish to be harboring the enemy."

It wasn't the first time Tom had heard such sentiments. In the past he'd dismissed them as a natural, albeit unfortunate, result of being at war. This was the first time they had been directed at someone he knew. "I believe I heard that Mrs. Gottlieb is an American," he said, hoping to diffuse Hank's anger.

It didn't work. Tom's landlord glared at him. "A piece of paper don't make no difference. That woman was born in Germany, and that means she's a German." Hank stared into the distance for a moment, then said, "I'll bet she's spying for the Kaiser, reporting everything that's happening here."

The idea was so preposterous that Tom had to force himself not to laugh. He did not doubt that espionage occurred on both sides, but he could not imagine what military significance Hank believed Canela held. The residents might buy Liberty Bonds and they might collect fruit pits for use in the soldiers' charcoal gas masks, but Tom suspected that was the extent of their involvement in the war, once they had sent their men to fight.

"Mrs. York strikes me as a good judge of character. As you said," he told Hank, trying to make the man understand that his fears were groundless, "there's no nonsense about her. If she trusts Mrs. Gottlieb, that's good enough for me."

Hank shook his head. "Don't say I didn't warn you just like I warned Martha." The sound of rattling dishes came through the open window, making Tom wonder how much of the conversation Linda Bradley had overheard and whether she shared her husband's opinions. "I can't understand why Martha would trust a German when they're the ones that killed her brother. They're the same ones my son and all the other red-blooded Americans are fighting." Hank tapped his pipe on his chair arm. "It's wrong letting them Germans stay here, and no one can tell me otherwise."

Though he tried to dismiss them, Hank Bradley's vitriolic words were still echoing in Tom's mind the next afternoon. How many other Americans, he wondered, felt the same way as Hank Bradley? They might claim that Tom didn't understand, because he wasn't fighting and didn't have any family serving in the Army, but they were wrong. Tom hated the war as much as anyone did. He hated the killing and the destruction. He hated the men whose decisions had led to the fighting. But he couldn't hate people whose sole crime was to have been born in another country.

Tom had said nothing to Martha when he had walked her to school, although it had been on the tip of his tongue to ask whether she was aware of the anti-German sentiment. He hadn't, though, because he hadn't wanted to spoil her morning. Now school was over for the day, and she was taking him on the first leg of their tour of the Friendliest Little Town in East Texas. Tom carried his camera and a supply of unexposed plates in his left hand, keeping

Martha on his right. Though she enunciated clearly, as he would have expected of a schoolteacher, he didn't want to miss a single word.

"This is the Canela Bank and Trust," she said, pointing to a light brick building on the northeast corner of Main and Broad Streets. Although not the tallest building in town, a distinction that was held by the church, the bank was one of the most impressive, with four columns in its façade. "My Great-grandfather Wentworth founded it," Martha continued. "It's been in the family ever since."

Tom looked at the building with more interest, trying to imagine the four generations who had made their living here. Had all the Wentworths been handsome, or had Martha's beauty come from her mother's side of the family? And had all the bankers been as sensible as she? The bank's obvious prosperity made Tom guess that was the case. "Who runs it now?" Theo was the obvious choice, but Theo was in France, presumably dead.

A shadow crossed Martha's face, and her eyes darkened. "Mr. Carter. He used to be the manager when my father was alive, but he retired when Theo took over. When my brother enlisted, he convinced Mr. Carter to come back temporarily." Martha pursed her lips. "I don't know what we'll do after the war."

"Then you don't share your sister's belief that Theo is alive? I thought that was why you still had a blue star."

"That was Emily's doing. She insisted that we not change the star." Martha laid her forefinger across her lips in a gesture Tom had come to realize meant she was trying to control her emotions. "I don't know what to think," Martha continued. "I want to believe that Emily's intuition is correct. She was always closer to Theo than Carolyn and I were, and she claims that twins know things that other siblings don't. I want to believe her, Tom, but I don't know if I can." Martha's expression was bleak as she said, "The

Army is convinced that he was with the rest of the battalion and that there were no survivors."

Two elderly women exited the bank, nodding to Martha. Though she greeted them politely and introduced him, Tom sensed that her thoughts were thousands of miles away in France, where her brother might or might not be alive. Tom wished he could offer consolation, but all he could say was, "Mistakes happen."

Martha nodded, setting a lock of silver blond hair bouncing against her cheek. "This whole war was a mistake. I wish it had never started."

"But it has, and now we're all fighting every day."

She looked up at him, those lovely turquoise eyes clouded with confusion. "What do you mean? The fighting is in Europe."

If only it were that simple. "It's here, too." When Martha started to protest, Tom continued, "I'll agree that it's a different kind of fighting, but it's still war. How else would you describe the anti-German sentiments?"

"You mean the fact that we're supposed to call hamburgers 'liberty burgers' and sauerkraut 'liberty cabbage'?"

She either hadn't heard Hank Bradley's opinions, or she was trying to ignore them. "I mean the hostility toward what people are calling hyphenated-Americans, including your friend Anna."

Martha frowned, then touched her finger to her lips again. "It's just a few people who feel that way."

So she did know about Hank. "I hope so. I didn't like what I heard." Even more, Tom hated the thought of what a group of people who felt as Hank did could do if provoked. He had seen peaceful gatherings turn ugly as one person fanned anger, converting ordinary citizens into a mob. It was not a pleasant prospect.

"Let me take your picture next to the bank," Tom said, deliberately changing the subject.

Though she moved closer to one of the columns, Martha shook her head. "I'm not going to agree, you know."

She would. She had to, because so much depended on her. "Wait until the pictures are developed. You can make your decision then."

"I told you I was stubborn."

"And I'm tenacious. Now that we agree on that, will you let me tell you why I think the Fourth of July Woman is important?"

She wrapped her arm around the column the way he'd suggested. "It won't change my mind, but I'll listen."

Tom opened the camera, checking that he had an unexposed plate. "You've probably read what it's like in the trenches." Men like journalist Grant Randall had told the Doughboys' stories far more eloquently than Tom could, but he had to try to make Martha understand what her picture would mean to the ordinary soldiers. "The men live for three things: the morning and evening stand-to when they get out of the trenches and breathe fresh air, and mail call. Of the three, I've heard that mail call is the most important. It's a reminder of home and why they're fighting." Tom focused the camera.

Martha was listening, and the way she had tipped her head was perfect. It would be a good picture, perhaps even good enough to be the Fourth of July Woman. "Men don't get mail every day, but they still need reminders of home, so they hang up photographs on the dirt walls of the trenches." Tom looked through the focusing hood, then released the shutter. "I want the Fourth of July Woman to be a photograph for all the men who don't have wives and sweethearts at home. I want her to be the symbol of the quintessential American woman." Martha's eyes widened and Tom pulled out the plate holder, reversing it so that he had unexposed film in the Graflex. "I want those men to be able to pretend that she's waiting for them at home," he continued. "The Fourth of July Woman's picture could be the one thing that saves a man's life."

Martha looked at him steadily, her expression one he'd never seen and could not classify. "It's a beautiful thought," she said at last, "but I'm not that woman."

"Yes, you are." She had to be.

Chapter Five

The morning was cooler than normal, with a pleasant breeze coming from the north. They stood in the shade of an ancient oak tree, its branches so dense that little light filtered through them. There was no reason why beads of perspiration should have formed on Tom's forehead, and yet they had. Martha stared at the man who in just a few minutes would enter the schoolhouse with her. He looked especially handsome this morning, his shirt freshly laundered, his cravat perfectly knotted, his suit brushed and pressed. If Martha had been asked to describe the ideal American man, she would have done nothing more than describe Tom Fleming and the way he looked this morning, all except for that moist forehead. He couldn't be nervous, could he?

As if he sensed her thoughts, Tom said, "I hope I don't disappoint you or the children."

For some inexplicable reason, the man whose pictures had delighted thousands of people was worried about facing thirty young children. "I can't imagine you disappointing anyone," Martha said, her voice as firm and reassuring as if she were speaking to one of her pupils. "The children are so excited about your visit that you wouldn't have to

do anything other than smile at them, and they'd be happy."
It had been difficult to get anyone to concentrate on lessons
yesterday, and only the threat of canceling Tom's appearance had motivated the class to complete their multiplica-
tion tables.

It was obvious Tom didn't believe her. "I've never done
this before," he admitted.

A momentary pang of regret swept through Martha.
When she'd asked him to address her pupils, she hadn't
considered the fact that a photographer probably had no
need to develop skills in public speaking. Furthermore, as
an only child, he had no nieces or nephews. Judging from
his reaction, he was uncomfortable around youngsters.
"They're only children," she said, continuing to use her
best school voice.

"But there are so many of them."

Martha reached forward and laid her hand on Tom's. It
might be inappropriate. Her mother would have frowned if
she had seen the gesture. Martha didn't care. What mattered
was easing Tom's nervousness. "You'll be perfect," she
said.

Faint color stained his neck. "Now you're embarrassing
me."

Martha merely smiled and opened the door to the schoolhouse. As she and Tom walked to the front of the room,
the children, who had been clamoring for Canela's celebrity
to visit them, fell silent.

"Boys and girls, we have a very special guest today."
Martha stood beside her desk, letting her gaze move from
one child to the next. "I know you'll be quiet while he talks
to us. At the end, if you're good, Mr. Fleming may answer
some questions."

A murmur of anticipation rippled through the classroom;
then there was silence. Tom placed the wooden trunk that
he'd been carrying on Martha's desk and took a step forward.

"Once upon a time," he said, his voice carrying clearly to the back of the room, "there was a little boy much like you." He gestured toward one of the children, then another, then a third. Martha stared, amazed. Tom might claim he was uncomfortable with children, but he appeared to have an intuitive knowledge of how to enthrall them. "The boy," Tom continued, "didn't know what he wanted to do when he grew up. His parents told him he could be a doctor or a lawyer or a teacher or a fireman or a policeman. He wasn't sure what he would like best. And then he discovered this." Tom reached behind him and pulled his camera out of the case. A collective sigh came from the children.

For the next few minutes, Tom talked about the camera itself, its parts and how it worked. He told them that it was made of mahogany covered with Moroccan leather and let each child peer into the focusing hood so that they could see that the image was right-side up. "In older cameras," he told them, "the images were upside down. What do you think the photographers did?"

Three hands shot into the air. "They stood on their heads," one boy suggested.

"No, but they sometimes wished they could. The truth is, they got used to it just the way you get used to holding a fork and knife the right way. It feels awkward at first, but then you get used to it."

Tom pulled out a plate holder and showed the children how it had two sides. "That means I can take two pictures very quickly." He continued by telling them how he developed and printed his photographs. Even the children who normally fidgeted were quiet, listening to Tom's explanations.

When he finished, Paul Anderson raised his hand. "Is it magic?"

Tom shook his head. "Some people think so, though." And he launched into a story of one of the tribes he'd met during his travels and how they'd been convinced he had captured their spirits inside the camera. "I call it a memory maker," Tom said. "People look at a photograph and remember the person or the place."

He reached into the case and pulled out several photographs. "What do you think when you see these?" he asked, initiating an animated discussion with the children as he showed them a picture of apple pie, another of an older man standing next to a finely carved desk, and a third that depicted a large brick building with a hundred or so men approaching its entrance. To Martha's surprise, though the students had a number of comments about each photograph, ranging from asking if the pie was as delicious as it looked to announcing that the building was too big for Main Street in Canela, no one asked where Tom had taken them. Instead, they seemed fascinated by the pictures themselves.

When at last he finished, Martha turned to the students. "If you have any questions, boys and girls, raise your hands."

At first no one spoke, then Helen Sempert raised her hand. "Will you tell us about your family, Mr. Fleming?"

Tom nodded and picked up the three pictures he'd shown them. "My parents live in Rochester, New York, not too far from Mr. Eastman's factory. That's the building in this photograph, and that's where my camera was made." Tom gestured toward the camera as he spoke. "My father makes furniture, and my mother bakes the best apple pies in New York State." He picked up the other two pictures. "Who do you think this is?" he asked, pointing to the man standing next to the desk.

"Your Pa!" the children cried in unison.

"And who made the pie?"

"Your Ma!"

As Tom nodded, the children giggled, obviously pleased that they'd guessed correctly.

Though Helen, who had asked the original question, appeared satisfied, May Gibson was not. She stared at Tom for a moment, then, her forehead furrowed with concentration, she said, "You didn't tell us about your wife."

Tom gave the little girl a quick smile. "That's because I don't have a wife."

May's forehead smoothed as she returned Tom's smile. "You should marry Mrs. York. She needs a husband."

Marry Mrs. York. The nonsensical words still reverberated through his brain even hours later. It was a ridiculous thought. Tom wouldn't deny that Martha York was an attractive woman. The truth was, she was a very attractive woman, perhaps the most attractive woman he'd met. He also wouldn't deny the allegation that Martha needed a husband. The sorrow and loneliness he saw reflected in her eyes—part of what had attracted him in the first place—said that she did. But just because she was attractive and needed a husband didn't mean he should marry her.

Tom shuddered as he leaned against the old oak tree. Marriage? Absurd! Preposterous! Marriage wasn't part of his plans. Marriage meant settling down, and that was something Tom had no intention of doing. How could the Peripatetic Photographer do his job if he stayed in one place? He couldn't. He would have to do something different. Tom wasn't ready for that; moreover, he wasn't convinced he ever would be.

The sound of children's laughter spilled out of the schoolhouse. Without even trying, Tom could picture Martha standing by the chalkboard, her lips curved in a sweet smile at her pupils' exuberance. This was where she belonged. Martha had roots here, and she was not the type of plant that transplanted easily. Tom, on the other hand, had no roots at all. Some people were happiest alone, moving from place to place, savoring the new experiences. He was one of those men. He knew that as well as he knew that the thought of marrying Martha York was totally, absolutely crazy.

He ought to leave Canela, and he would . . . just as soon
as he got the photographs he needed and just as soon as he
convinced Martha to let him use them. That was the only
reason he was back at the schoolhouse, waiting for her to
come out. It had nothing to do with wanting to see her
smile and wondering whether she was as disturbed by the
children's suggestion as he was. It certainly had nothing to
do with the sinking feeling that had lodged in his stomach
when he had thought of Martha York remarrying.

"Thank you again," Martha said as they began to walk
toward the center of town. Though she had blushed slightly
when she saw him, she made no reference to the little girl's
ridiculous proposal. *Proposal!* Tom grimaced. That was a
word he should expunge from his vocabulary, particularly
today. He didn't want to think about proposals, marriage
and Martha all in the same sentence.

"You were the only thing the children wanted to talk
about. They were more excited about your visit than they
were about the carousel." Frank Patton had agreed to send
one of his merry-go-rounds to Canela, and the Independence Day committee had quickly ratified the idea. Tom
was glad about that. It felt good to have been able to re-
solve one of Martha's problems. That had been easy compared to facing thirty curious children and their
preposterous suggestion.

"Half the class is convinced they'll be photographers
when they grow up." Martha was speaking as if nothing
out of the ordinary had happened. It was clear that she had
dismissed the idea of a pro—. Tom shook his head. He
wouldn't use that word. It was clear that Martha had dismissed the absurd idea the instant it had been spoken. It
was only he who had spent the past four hours and 37
minutes remembering how a little girl with dark brown
braids had made his stomach plummet and his heart race
with her ridiculous suggestion.

"We pulled out a map of the world and traced your travels." Martha's voice was low and sweet. It appeared that she had regarded today's events as perfectly normal. Tom would take his cue from her. He would pretend that nothing out of the ordinary had occurred.

"I enjoyed being with the children." It was the truth. Even better, it was a safe topic. Tom would talk about the children and nothing else.

Martha gave him a long appraising look. They were walking down Oak Street as they did each afternoon. It was, Tom reflected, one of the prettiest streets in Canela, almost as attractive as Chestnut, the street where Martha lived. "You didn't expect to enjoy it, did you?"

"Was it that obvious that I thought medieval torture would be more pleasant?" When she shrugged, Tom continued. "I'm not used to children, but I found it interesting—and enlightening—to see the world through their eyes." All except for that part of their world that said he should marry their schoolteacher.

"Anna says they're what keep her young, and I have to agree with her."

"Because you're so old." Tom couldn't help scoffing at the idea. Martha was young and attractive and . . . He shook his head. Those were thoughts he should not be entertaining.

"Some days I feel as if I'm a hundred," she admitted.

"Then I have just the cure for you. Mr. Martin told me there's a dinner dance at the country club tomorrow night." It had become a habit, stopping in Mr. Martin's store each morning after he left Martha at school. Tom found that he enjoyed the older man's wry sense of humor, though he'd been unable to convince him that he had not been sent by the Army. Still, the shopkeeper's unique view of life brightened the hours that Martha was in school.

"I'd be pleased if you would go to the dance with me." Given the direction his thoughts had strayed all day, he shouldn't have suggested it, but the simple fact was, Tom needed to spend more time with Martha if he was going to get the perfect photograph. That was the reason he had invited her. The *only* reason.

"You like to keep Canela's gossip active, don't you?" The amusement on Martha's face told him her protest was a pro forma one.

"You can consider it part of your tour guide service." Tom realized it was important he tell her that. After what had happened that morning, he didn't want her to think there was anything—he stumbled over the word—anything *romantic* about the invitation. For Pete's sake, it wasn't as if he were courting her. This was a purely business proposal. Tom frowned. There it was, that word he'd vowed to expunge from his vocabulary.

"Does that mean you're planning to take pictures there?" Her voice was so matter-of-fact that Tom realized his concerns had been groundless. Martha hadn't misunderstood his motives.

"Of the country club? Of course."

It was half the truth, and Martha seemed to know it. "And of me?"

He wouldn't lie. "Yes, but I won't use any photographs without your permission." When she nodded her understanding, he asked, "Will you go to dinner with me?"

This time her nod was enthusiastic. "I'd like that."

So, Tom suspected, would he.

It was silly to feel so excited about a dinner invitation, just as it was silly to have been so embarrassed by May Gibson's ridiculous suggestion. Martha laid her fingers on her cheeks, trying to cool the heat that rose to them, though it had been a full day since May had uttered those disturbing words. She couldn't blame the girl. May was a child, a mere eight years old. Of course she saw things in simple terms. In her world, everyone got married. She hadn't meant any harm. May didn't understand that Martha wasn't the type of woman a man like Tom Fleming would marry. She didn't understand concepts like love and attraction and wanting the same things in life. In May's world, everything led to happily ever after. In Martha's world, things were far more complex, and happily ever after was something that happened to other people.

Martha poured water into her wash basin and dipped a cloth into it. Perhaps a cool compress would help dissipate the blush. It was true that she found Tom attractive. Who wouldn't, when the man was one of the most beautiful creatures on earth? It was true that she enjoyed his company more than any man's that she could remember. It was true that since Tom Fleming had come to Canela, the emptiness that had been part of Martha's life for so long seemed to have lessened. It was also true that today for the first time since her marriage she had wakened thinking of someone other than Henry. All that was true. What wasn't true was that she would marry Tom, even if he asked. Which he would not. A man like Tom Fleming could have his choice of women. He would choose a woman like him: cosmopolitan, well-traveled, beautiful. He would never ask an ordinary small-town schoolteacher like Martha to marry him.

Martha dipped the cloth again and wrung it out. The way her face felt, she'd need a piece of ice to cool it. How foolish! Tom wouldn't ask her to marry him, and even if he did, she wouldn't accept. Of course she wouldn't. Martha had been married once, and she knew that marriage was not necessarily the start of happily ever after. She had loved and lost once, and she had no intention of enduring that kind of pain again.

Which was why it made no sense that she was now standing in front of her armoire, frowning at every frock it held. The lilac one was pretty. Henry had complimented her when she wore that one. And the pale mauve dress was one Carolyn had said suited Martha. She could wear either of them and be perfectly well dressed for an evening at the country club. Why, then, did she find herself unwilling to consider those possibilities?

Martha gave the contents of her armoire one last look, then closed the door and reached for her hat. It was probably foolish, but she would do it, anyway.

"Good morning, Miss Bloom," Martha said a few minutes later as she opened the door to The Canela Dress Emporium.

"Good morning." The elderly proprietor rose from the rocking chair. Tall and thin, she was a striking figure. Though she continued to wear her hair in a pompadour, a style that had been out of fashion for years, Miss Bloom's dress was a copy of the latest style from Paris. She smiled at Martha. "You're looking right pretty today."

What Martha was feeling was right foolish, though she wouldn't admit it to Ida Bloom or anyone else in Canela. She might not even tell her sisters about her visit to Canela's best—and only—seamstress. "I would like a new dress." Martha looked around the room. It might simply be her imagination, but she thought there were fewer dresses hanging in the four alcoves than she had seen the last time.

Ida Bloom gave Martha's shirtwaist and skirt a professional appraisal. "For school?"

There was no reason why Martha's face should flush as she said, "No. I wanted something fancier," just as there was no reason that the blush should deepen when Ida Bloom nodded and said, "I see." There was nothing for Miss Bloom to see. Nothing at all.

With an agility that belied her seven decades, the emporium's proprietor walked to the other side of the room and pulled a frock off its hanger. "I think you'll like this," she said as she motioned Martha toward the cheval mirror and held a turquoise gown in front of her. Though the dress had none of the ruffles and furbelows that some women preferred, Martha knew that the simple style would flatter her.

"It's beautiful."

"I made it from a French pattern," Ida Bloom told Martha as she helped her slide the gown over her head. The dress itself was fashioned from deep turquoise silk, but what made it special was the light turquoise chiffon that formed the elbow-length sleeves and the overskirt. "It's called a handkerchief hem." Ida Bloom gestured toward the bottom of the overskirt that ended in a series of points six inches above the hem of the main dress. She handed Martha a wide sash, indicating that it was to be worn with the ends trailing in the back.

As Martha stared at her reflection in the cheval glass, she had to agree with Miss Bloom's assessment. She did like the dress, for it was more beautiful than any gown she had ever owned. The color was perfect, and the softly draped overskirt made Martha feel as if she were a princess, preparing for a special ball.

"He won't be able to take his eyes off you."

Martha turned to stare at the proprietor.

"Who do you mean?"

Ida Bloom straightened the sash. "Why, that photographer, of course. Everyone in Canela knows he's sparking you."

"He's not!" It was a ridiculous allegation, as preposterous as May's suggestion that Tom marry Martha, as absurd as the fact that Martha's cheeks were once more bright red. "Tom's here to take pictures of Canela, that's all." Why was everyone in this town obsessed with the thought of marriage?

Ida Bloom chuckled softly. "You can't fool an old woman."

"You're not old." Though Martha knew that Miss Bloom was over seventy, she was so active that she seemed decades younger.

"Yes, my dear, I am old. That's why I'm closing the emporium at the end of June." Her smile was bittersweet, as though the decision had been a difficult one. "A person gets tired of working."

Closing the emporium? Martha stared at the older woman, trying to accept what she had heard. The store had been in this location for as long as Martha could remember. Her first memory of it was being five or six years old and coming into the shop with her mother. At the time, Martha had been thrilled by the fact that she and Mother had come alone, leaving Carolyn and Emily at home. Martha remembered feeling grown up as she watched Mother try on dresses in front of the same cheval glass that now stood in front of Martha. The Canela Dress Emporium and Miss Bloom were important parts of the town. Though so much else had changed, they'd remained constant. Surely that wouldn't end.

"What will we do without you?" Martha demanded, her heart aching at the thought of Ida Bloom's retirement. Canela simply wouldn't be the same.

The white-haired woman's eyes twinkled. "Don't worry, Martha. Even if the shop is closed, I'll still make your wedding dress."

Wedding dress! Miss Bloom was as bad as May Gibson. "But—"

The dressmaker interrupted Martha's protest. "You come see me when you and that handsome photographer set the date. I'll be waiting."

It was ridiculous. Absolutely, positively ridiculous.

Perhaps it was her imagination, but the country club looked prettier than ever when she and Tom walked into it that evening. The white linen that covered the tables in the main dining room seemed snowier than normal, and the string quartet that had replaced the orchestra now that most of the musicians were thousands of miles away, fighting for their country, sounded better than normal. Even the flowers, which Martha had had to hurry to finish in time, seemed to smell sweeter than normal.

It was silly, of course, to think that everything seemed better because of the expression she had seen in Tom's eyes when she had walked out of her front door. His eyes had scanned her from the top of her head to the tip of her shoes, seeming to take in every detail of the new dress. And then he'd smiled, a smile of pure appreciation, before he'd pulled out his camera.

"Beautiful," he'd said.

"Thank you. I thought it was a pretty frock."

Tom's chuckle had warmed her heart as much as his smile did. "I wasn't referring to the dress, although it's nice, too. No, Martha, you're the one who's beautiful."

And, oddly enough, she had felt beautiful.

They stood in the doorway, waiting for the maitre d' to escort them to their table. As Martha had expected, every eye in the room had turned toward them when they had arrived. She couldn't blame the other patrons. After all, Tom wasn't simply a famous visitor; he was also a very handsome visitor, especially tonight when he wore formal clothing. The dark coat and white linen highlighted his blond hair and somehow made his eyes seem even deeper blue than normal. Though the camera that he carried in his left hand should have looked incongruous in this setting, it did not. Instead, it served as a reminder that Tom Fleming was an extraordinary man, not simply breathtakingly handsome, but also supremely talented.

"It's fancier than I imagined," Tom said, his eyes assessing the room with what Martha had come to consider his professional eye. Though she couldn't quite explain it, something in Tom's expression changed when he was considering how to photograph a room . . . or a person.

"I told you it was a nice town," she said as took the chair the maitre d' had pulled out for her. Once they'd started walking through the dining room, normal conversation had resumed, as if the other patrons wanted to mask their curiosity.

Tom glanced at the menu, then said, "Canela seems to be prosperous, even though it's wartime."

The town had been lucky, and Martha knew it. But now, she feared, that luck might have turned. All afternoon while she had been arranging flowers, she had thought about Miss Bloom's decision. "I'm worried about Mr. Martin," she admitted.

Tom gave their order to the elderly waiter. "Have sales dropped a lot?" he asked when the man was out of earshot.

Martha shrugged. "Mr. Martin doesn't say much, but with all the men gone, I can't imagine that sales are more than half what they were a year ago. And now that Miss Bloom is closing the Dress Emporium . . ."

"Surely you don't think that's a result of the war."

Martha didn't. There were as many women in Canela as before the war, and with the men gone, many of them who had previously made their own clothing had no time to sew. Ida Bloom's business was a thriving one. Perhaps that was part of the problem. Perhaps she was too busy.

"She says she's tired of working."

Tom handed Martha the butter plate and watched while she spread only a thin coating on her roll, mindful of the government's admonition to save fats for the war effort. "How does Miss Bloom's retirement affect Mr. Martin?"

"He's her landlord, and now he won't have the rent." Martha broke off another piece of bread. "I can't think of anyone in Canela who needs a shop on Main Street."

Tom looked up from his salad, his blue eyes reflecting surprise. "You're amazing, Martha."

It was her turn to be surprised. "Why do you say that?" Like *beautiful, amazing* was not a word Martha associated with herself.

"It seems that you've taken on responsibility for everyone in Canela. I've heard of town fathers. In this case, I'd say that you were the town's mother."

Spearing a piece of lettuce, Martha said, "You sound as if you think there's something wrong with that."

Tom shook his head. "I'm not saying it's wrong; it's simply outside my range of experience."

The string quartet, which had taken a brief break, were tuning their instruments. Martha knew the waiters would delay bringing the next course until the quartet had played one song, for the interlude had been a tradition for as long as the country club had been in existence.

"Haven't you ever felt responsible for others?" Martha asked Tom. Although he wasn't like her, the oldest child who took responsibility for the younger ones, surely Tom had had at least one protégé when he'd been growing up.

He laid down his salad fork and looked at her. "I found life's a lot easier if you're responsible only for yourself."

The response surprised Martha so much that she blinked. "Easier isn't necessarily better." She had gained so much by caring for her siblings and volunteering for various town committees. Didn't Tom understand that she didn't just live here, she was part of the town, just as she was part of a family? Anna had once told Martha that they were two of a kind, women who gave of themselves. At the time Martha had protested, telling Anna that she felt she received more than she gave. Friendship, love, a sense of belonging— those were all gifts the town and her family had bestowed on her. Tom had missed so much.

"I don't disagree with you." Tom slid his chair back and rose as the music began. "Would you like to dance?"

Though she suspected he had suggested the dance as a means of changing the subject, Martha did not refuse. Dancing was one of her favorite activities. It was also one of the things she and Henry had enjoyed doing together. Even before they'd become engaged and then married, they had been a couple on the dance floor. Some had even called them Canela's Castles, referring to the famous dancing couple, Irene and Vernon Castle. Martha loved to dance. Unfortunately, since the war had begun, she had had few opportunities. She took Tom's hand and led the way onto the dance floor. Seconds later, she was in his arms and they were moving in time to the music.

Dancing with Tom was nothing like dancing with Henry. Martha and Henry had learned to dance together, and they'd done it almost instinctively. From the first beat, it was evident that Tom was not the skilled partner Martha's husband had been. Whereas Henry had rarely missed a step and never trod on her toes, Tom was obviously not an experienced dancer. His movements were more tentative than Henry's had been, almost as if he were doing this for the first time. Tom bumped her toes more than once and swung her around on the wrong beat. And yet, despite his lack of expertise, Martha could not remember a dance she had enjoyed more.

It felt good to be held in Tom Fleming's arms. It felt right to glide across the room with him. It felt wonderful to be his partner. If only the dance would never end!

He shouldn't be doing this. It was after midnight, and any sane person would be asleep. A sane person wouldn't have draped his window with a thick blanket and replaced the light bulb with a red light. He wouldn't be pouring developer into a tray, taking care not to splash any on the floor. But a sane person probably wouldn't feel the way Tom did, excitement mingling with fear. It was always this way when he developed pictures.

While his hands moved almost mechanically, repeating the process he'd done so many times, dipping plates into the chemicals, checking them to see whether they were ready to be rinsed and fixed, Tom's mind continued to whirl. Though he had had high hopes for the evening, those hopes had paled against the reality. It had started when

Martha had stepped through her front door, looking more beautiful than any one woman had a right to in that dress the color of a tropical sea. She had been so beautiful that for a moment Tom had felt as tongue-tied as a schoolboy. What could he say, what could he do when faced with that perfection? Fortunately, Tom had had his camera with him, and instinct had taken over. He had taken a photograph of Martha standing on the porch. It was that photograph that filled him with excitement and fear—excitement over the possibility that this might be the one he wanted, fear that it wasn't as good as he'd hoped.

Tom held the first plate up to the light. Not yet. It needed another minute or two. While he waited, he let his mind return to the country club. Who would have guessed it would feel so good to dance with Martha York? He had invited her onto the floor because he knew it was expected. A couple did not attend a dinner dance without enduring at least one episode of shuffling around on polished wood. Mr. Martin had told Tom that Martha had always enjoyed dancing. He had told Tom that Martha's husband—a man Mr. Martin praised so often that Tom had begun to think of him as "Saint Henry"—had been a superb dancer.

Though he knew he was far from a skilled partner, Tom was willing to try a dance—maybe even two—if it would bring Martha some pleasure. He knew he couldn't compare to her husband, but he wasn't even going to try. A man had to know his limits, and perfect dancing was outside Tom's. He figured he could endure a dance or two for Martha. What he hadn't expected was that the experience of dancing with her would be so enjoyable that he wanted to repeat it as often as possible.

Tom had danced the Castle Gavotte before. He knew the steps. He knew the music. What he hadn't known was that a dance could be pleasurable. While others seemed to glide effortlessly to the music, Tom's hearing loss meant that he had to concentrate, sometimes straining to hear the notes

over the sounds of shoes echoing on the floor and the danc-
ers' conversations. As a result, *pleasure* was not a word he
used in the same sentence with *dancing*. It was a duty,
nothing more. To Tom's surprise, dancing with Martha was
different. Dancing with her was enjoyable. More than that,
it was exciting. While they'd been dancing, he'd forgotten
that he was in Canela to photograph the Fourth of July
Woman. He'd forgotten that war was being waged on the
other side of the ocean. He'd forgotten everything except
the delight of holding a beautiful blond with turquoise eyes
in his arms.

Tom watched as the images began to appear. This was
his favorite part of developing photographs. It was as close
to magic as anything he'd ever experienced. He squinted,
looking at first one, then the next. Not bad. All right. They
were decent photographs, but none of them stirred him the
way they should. They weren't pedestrian. Sidney would
agree that they were good enough for the *Gainey Gazette*,
but Tom wasn't satisfied. He knew he could do better. The
Fourth of July Woman had to be better than these.

His mouth suddenly dry, he pulled out the photograph
of Martha on the porch and stared at it, not quite believing
his eyes. A second later a shaft of purely visceral pleasure
swept through Tom. This was it! This was the picture he'd
been seeking. This was his Fourth of July Woman!

She stood next to a climbing vine, and though it appeared
that she had just sniffed the flowers, her eyes were fixed
on the distance, a haunting smile on her face. That smile
said that she was waiting for someone and that that someone was very, very special. Her lips curved upwards, her
eyes reflecting longing and anticipation and something else,
something that could only be called love.

It was perfect! Tom closed his eyes, imagining the men
in the trenches seeing Martha's picture. They'd dream of
her, and when they left the trenches to fight the enemy,
they'd remember her and the promise of happiness in that

smile. They'd remember Martha, and they'd come back to the trenches, determined that they would live to return home to a woman like her, a woman who promised a lifetime of happily ever after. Tom chuckled with delight. This was what he had envisioned from the very beginning. This was his Fourth of July Woman.

His fatigue forgotten, Tom rinsed the plates and dipped them in fixer. By morning they would be dry, ready for him to print them. He would make an extra print of this one so that he could leave it with Martha. He owed her that much for salvaging his career. Tom wouldn't consider the possibility that she would refuse. Surely when Martha saw her photograph, she would let him use it. She had to. As soon as she did, Tom would put it in the mail to Sidney. The man was waiting for this picture.

It wasn't only the difficulty of placing long-distance telephone calls that made Tom hesitate to call his editor. The last time they'd spoken, Sidney had been adamant, insisting that Tom deliver on his promise and that he do so quickly. It had been a far-from-pleasant conversation, and so when he'd arrived in Canela, rather than calling, Tom had sent Sidney a telegram, telling him he'd found the perfect woman but didn't yet have the perfect photograph. Now he did. If only she'd agree.

It was early afternoon when Tom slid the prints into a large envelope and drove to Martha's house. She had to be there. She had to agree. Tom's future depended on her answer. His heart beat rapidly as he climbed the porch steps.

"I have the first set of photographs," he said when she opened the door.

"Good afternoon, Tom. It's nice to see you." Even more than her greeting, Martha's amused smile made Tom realize he'd been so excited that he'd forgotten the social amenities.

"You're looking lovely today." She was. The dark blue dress with its white collar and cuffs highlighted her hair and somehow made her cheeks look especially rosy. Or perhaps it was the effort of restraining her laughter that brought color to her face.

"I haven't changed my mind about letting you use them," she said, "but I'd like to see your photographs."

Martha took a seat on the swing, extending her hand for the envelope and motioning him to sit beside her. But he couldn't. Instead he stood where he had an unobstructed view of her face. He wanted to watch her, to see her reaction. Tom wouldn't believe that once she saw The Photograph, as he'd begun to call it in his mind, she would refuse to let him use it.

Tom had interspersed photographs of her with the others, wanting Martha to see every picture he'd taken. She looked briefly at the first photograph, the one of her in the Model T, dismissing it as if it were of no importance. It was a good picture, but that didn't appear to interest her. Other photographs of her met the same fate. But then she slowed.

"This is wonderful!" she cried, pointing to a picture of Mr. Martin standing at the door to his store, as if willing someone to enter. "I've seen him look exactly like that so many times. You've captured him perfectly."

The next picture was The Photograph. To Tom's dismay, Martha made no comment, simply glanced at it and turned to the next one. But then her expression changed, a smile illuminating her face as she stared at her friend's image. "Look at the way Anna's head is cocked while she listens to May. You can see that she's interested and that she cares about the girl. That's Anna, and you've captured her perfectly."

Martha looked at the rest of the pictures, then laid them on her lap. "Tom, these are the best pictures I've ever seen. Do you know what you've done here?" Her eyes sparkled with enthusiasm, and her smile was joyous. "You're not just taking pictures of Canela; you're telling the town's story. It's wonderful!"

Chapter Six

Tom stared at her for a moment, his mind whirling as he considered the possibility. It was an ordinary afternoon in Canela. People strolled down the streets; clouds flirted with the sun; birds sang to their mates. When he had come to Martha's house, he had had a single goal: convince her to let him use The Photograph. If she had, the ordinary afternoon would have been transformed into a special one. Martha hadn't agreed—not yet—but she had made an intriguing suggestion.

Tom looked down at the photographs that had excited her. All he had wanted were pictures of his Fourth of July Woman. He had taken the others simply because taking photographs was what he did and because he had hoped that the fact that she wasn't the only subject would help Martha relax. He had had no intention of doing anything special with those pictures. If they had in some way told a story, it was purely accidental.

Tom raised a hand to his right ear, remembering the day he had heard the thunder. He, more than most people, had good reason to know that accidents could have unexpected—and very positive—results. This afternoon was a perfect example. Martha had said many things, but one word out of all of them had triggered a response deep within him. That one word had suggested a possibility he had not considered. If luck was with him, that one word might restore his professional reputation.

"It wasn't a conscious effort to tell a story," he admitted as he took the seat next to Martha, "but you might be right."

There was no question about it. Martha's unusual turquoise eyes sparkled with amusement. "My students will tell you I'm always right." She leafed through the photographs again, stopping to study several. "These are hauntingly beautiful," she said, her voice low and filled with something that sounded almost like reverence. "You've taken ordinary people doing ordinary things," she continued, "and somehow you've made them look extraordinary. I don't know what to say, Tom, other than that I feel as if you've created poetry. These are simply beautiful."

What was beautiful was Martha and the way her lips curved into a smile. Because he was seated with his left ear closer to her, Tom had turned so that he could watch her lips as she spoke, and he'd seen not only her smile but the sparkle in her eyes.

"Will you let me use the pictures?" he asked. Though he might have argued that his agreement not to use photographs without Martha's permission applied only to the pictures he took of her, Tom wanted to be certain she approved of his plan. "When you talked about telling a story, it made me think of the rotogravure section," he said, referring to the supplement to the Sunday newspaper that featured a series of photographs with a single subject. Normally a number of photographers contributed to a single rotogravure. If Sidney approved, this one would be different. "I want to propose a section on Canela," Tom explained. "The papers have all been featuring the battlegrounds. What I'd like to do is show a typical American town and how it has been changed by the war."

Martha's response was instantaneous. "You'll make Canela famous!"

She sounded as if she approved, but Tom would leave nothing to chance. "Do you object? The fame will last only a short time." He knew that, while some people saved the rotogravures and referred back to them, those people were in the minority. For most, the pictures were enjoyed for one week until the next ones were published. For more permanent souvenirs, people collected stereographs. A special camera took two virtually identical images next to each other on a single card. When viewed with a stereoscope, the image appeared to be three-dimensional. Even though Tom preferred ordinary photographs which did not require a special viewer, there was no denying either stereographs' popularity or the fact that they captured more details than rotogravures did.

"Heavens, no, I don't mind if you use the pictures. I think it's a wonderful idea!"

Though it was the answer Tom wanted, Martha's response puzzled him. "I don't understand why you don't care that thousands of people will see pictures of your hometown and know it by name, but you won't let me use your photograph, even though you would be anonymous."

The shadow that crossed Martha's face could not be blamed on clouds, for the sun shone clearly. "That's different." Her tone left no doubt that she would not change her mind. No matter what he said or did, Martha did not want her picture made public.

"Won't you tell me why?" From everything Tom had heard and his own observations of her, he knew that Martha York was not a woman who did things capriciously. She was a woman who gave freely of herself—except where her picture was concerned. Though he might not agree with it, Tom was certain Martha had a reason for denying him permission to use the photographs. He wanted to learn that reason and why her expression became so bleak whenever she thought of being the Fourth of July Woman. It was more than curiosity, more even than trying to understand why she was putting roadblocks in his way. Most of all, Tom wanted to understand what had made Martha the way she was, for if he understood, perhaps he could find a way to ease her sorrow.

As she shook her head, refusing to explain her reason, Tom pulled The Photograph from the pile. "Look at this," he said, pointing to her image. "This is precisely how I envisioned the Fourth of July Woman." Tom was a modest man, not given to hyperbole, but he knew that this wasn't simply a good picture; it was a great one.

Although she had previously dismissed the pictures of herself, this time Martha stared at the photograph, her eyes narrowed as she studied the print. "I don't see anything special about it," she said at last.

"Then you must be blind." Tom tried to control his frustration. "Martha, I've taken hundreds of pictures, and I tell you, this is the best one. It's perfect. The lighting, the composition, and most of all, the subject. Everything is just the way it should be." He fixed his gaze on her, willing her to understand. He wanted this photograph to be printed, not just because of what it would mean to his career, but even more important, because of what it would mean to the men in the trenches. They were the reason he'd suggested the idea to Sidney; they were the reason he'd driven so many miles, searching for the right woman.

Martha's eyes clouded with what appeared to be anguish. Though he did not want to cause her any pain, Tom couldn't stop now. He had to make her understand why the Fourth of July Woman was so important. Tom touched the photo, drawing Martha's attention to her image. "Every man who sees this will fall in love with you, even if only a little bit." When Martha shook her head, denying the possibility, Tom nodded. "In his mind, he'll realize it's a fantasy, but his heart will know that you exist and that you're back here, waiting. The belief that there's a woman like you waiting for him to come home to will help keep him alive."

Martha closed her eyes, and the way her lips trembled made Tom think she was fighting tears. "It won't help," she said in a voice that wavered.

An older couple walked down the street, and for a moment Tom feared they were coming to visit Martha. Fortunately, they did nothing more than wave. Martha waved back, blinking furiously to keep the tears from tumbling down her cheeks. Tom hated it when women cried. There was something about tears that made him feel helpless, and that was not a feeling he enjoyed. He ought to change the subject, but he didn't, for he knew that tears or no tears, he was close to learning the reason for Martha's refusal, and that was important.

"Help me understand why you feel that way," he said, trying to keep his voice low and even.

She was silent for a moment, and Tom feared she would not answer. Then she said, her expression as bleak as a November day, "Because I didn't save Henry, and I didn't save my father."

Though Tom had suspected that Martha's refusal was in some way connected to her husband's death, the words still surprised him. They were speaking of photographs, yet she said *I*. That surprised Tom, as did the reference to her father. What role did he play?

"When he left," Martha continued, "Henry carried a photograph of me on our wedding day. He said he'd wear it near his heart and that it would keep him safe." As tears spilled from her eyes, she brushed them away. "It didn't. Henry was killed on the first sortie he flew."

The pain in Martha's voice was so raw that it wrenched Tom's heart as nothing had ever done. "I wish there were something I could say to comfort you." Though it was irrational to believe that her photograph had in any way contributed to her husband's death, naught would be gained by telling her that. The woman's pain was so deep that Tom feared that nothing would ever heal it. Some long-dead Roman had said that time heals all wounds. If he had met Martha York, he might have qualified his statement. Time didn't appear to be helping her.

"You mentioned your father," he said softly. Though he did not want to deepen her anguish, Tom needed to know the whole story.

"My parents were stricken with influenza soon after Henry was killed." Martha's voice was as bleak as a Northern winter. "Mama died, and Daddy was so ill that I feared he'd be next. It was late at night. The others were asleep, and I was reading to Daddy. All at once, he insisted that I make him a cup of tea. I didn't want to, but when I told him I couldn't leave him alone, he said I should put my wedding picture where he could see it. That way he wouldn't be alone." Martha's voice cracked. "It was only a few minutes, but by the time I came back with the tea, he was gone." She looked at Tom, those lovely turquoise eyes shimmering with tears. "Don't you see, Tom? My picture won't help anyone. It brings nothing but sorrow."

Tom stretched out his hand and laid it over Martha's, hoping that she would recognize the gesture as an attempt to comfort her. His own mother, who was still very much alive and prone to dispensing advice to her only son, had told him numerous times that a gentle touch could heal things that no doctor's medicines could. While he couldn't explain Henry's death, Tom suspected that Martha's father had known his time was close and had wanted to spare her the pain of watching him draw his last breath. Instead, the man had inadvertently deepened her wounds.

Martha pulled her hand away, as if Tom's fingers had burned her, and as she did, he saw the glint of light on gold. Her wedding band. While some widows removed their rings after the traditional year of mourning, Martha had not. It was, Tom suspected, more than symbolism. It appeared that in her heart, Martha still considered herself married.

The pain that shot through Tom surprised him with its intensity. It felt as if a huge fist were clenching his heart, squeezing the life from it, as he thought of Martha's love for Henry. Love like that was rare. Tom knew that, just as he knew it was ridiculous to be jealous of a man who'd been dead for over three years. It made no sense, and yet Tom couldn't help wishing that someone loved him the way Martha had loved Henry. Life would be wonderful if he had a wife like Martha.

Tom blinked. What on earth had sent that thought into his brain? It had been more than two days since the school-girl had blurted out her absurd suggestion. Surely he'd forgotten it by now. The fact was, Tom didn't want a wife, even one as beautiful and charming and, yes, as loveable as Martha. He was not planning to marry, not now and perhaps not ever.

"I'll need more pictures if I'm going to do a full roto-gravure section." Tom seized the topic in a desperate attempt to forget wives and wedding bands. "You've seen what I've taken so far. Do you have any suggestions for other subjects?"

The twin furrows between Martha's eyes disappeared. She, too, appeared to appreciate the change of topic, although, Tom suspected, for different reasons. Martha's thoughts were of the past; his dealt with an impossible future. "We're having our school play in two weeks," she said. "Can you stay that long?"

He shouldn't. Tom knew that. It was sheer proximity that was causing him to think of Martha, marriage and himself in the same sentence. The obvious cure was distance. He ought to take a few more pictures, then leave Canela far behind. Instead, Tom found himself nodding. "Sidney—

that's my editor—is always impatient, but I think he'll understand."

And maybe Sidney would be so happy with the pictures of Canela that he'd agree there was no reason to have a Fourth of July Woman. After all, Sidney hadn't thought much of the idea when Tom had first proposed it. It had only been after weeks of badgering that Sidney had agreed to consider Tom's picture. Though he hated to abandon the idea of the Fourth of July Woman, Tom saw no alternative. Martha would never agree to let him use her photo, and now that he'd seen her, he knew no one else would satisfy him. Tom would rather have no Fourth of July Woman than settle for second best.

The rotogravure would be the answer to all his problems. He would focus on the town and forget just how attractive one of its residents was. He could do that. Of course he could.

Martha couldn't help smiling as she polished her shoes the next morning. Polishing shoes was not something she enjoyed. It was a messy task, and no matter how much she brushed them, when she did the work on them, her shoes never shone the way they had when Theo had helped her. But today it didn't matter. Even though she'd spilled a bit of black on the floor, she was still smiling.

The reason wasn't hard to find. Tom's idea of featuring Canela in the *Gainey Gazette* was a brilliant one. Martha had always believed that her hometown was special, and this would prove it. Thousands and thousands of people would see what she found so appealing about The Friendliest Little Town in East Texas.

She had stayed up late last night, thinking of places and people Tom ought to photograph, and she was anxious to discuss them with him. It was odd, but Martha could not remember ever being so excited. It was, of course, the thought of the rotogravure that excited her. It wasn't the fact that Tom Fleming was planning to stay in Canela for at least two more weeks. Oh, it was true that she enjoyed his company. He was easy to talk to, and there were times when Martha felt he understood what she was thinking even without voicing the words. She had never had that experience with anyone else. It was, she guessed, similar to the connection that Emily claimed she and Theo had, but that was puzzling in itself. While it was logical that twins would share something special, Tom wasn't Martha's twin. He wasn't even her brother. There was no reason for them to be, as Emily would say, on the same wavelength.

As she stirred a pot of oatmeal, Martha pondered the changes she'd experienced since the day Tom Fleming drove his Model T into town. She couldn't explain why she felt the way she did. All she knew was that when she was with Tom, she felt different than she had at any other time in her life. If she had had to pick a single word to describe the way she felt, Martha would have said *alive*. When she was with Tom, she felt as if everything that happened before she met him had been a prelude, and now she was really living. Flowers smelled sweeter; birds' songs were more melodic; even the breeze felt softer since Tom had arrived. It was exhilarating, unexpected, and—unfortunately—transitory. Though she might wish otherwise, Tom would be gone in just a few weeks, and life would return to normal. Martha had always prized normality. Why, then, did it suddenly sound boring?

"You're famous," Anna announced as Martha entered the schoolhouse. Though it was unusual for Anna to arrive before Martha, this morning Martha had been five minutes late. Those extra five minutes had been spent with Tom, reviewing the people and places she had put on her list for him to photograph. He had seemed intrigued by them but had cautioned Martha that everything depended on his editor. If Sidney approved the idea, Tom would continue taking pictures. If not . . . Though he had not completed the sentence, Martha knew that Tom would have no reason to remain in Canela if he were not developing a rotogravure section.

"Famous?" Martha raised an eyebrow in response to Anna's statement. Fame, as she had told Tom, was not something she sought. He had seemed to understand that, although she sensed that he had not fully understood why she wouldn't let him use her photograph. After he'd left, Martha had looked at the copy he'd given her, trying to understand why he thought it was so good. She had failed to see anything more than an ordinary picture of an ordinary woman. Martha couldn't believe that her face would inspire anyone and she wouldn't—oh, no she wouldn't—take the chance that she was a jinx, that her photograph would have the same effect on others that it had had on Henry and her father, that instead of keeping them safe, it had somehow contributed to their deaths. That was why when Theo had left, though he'd talked about taking a photograph of the whole family with him, Martha had persuaded him that memories were better than pieces of cardboard.

Drawing her attention back to the present, Anna pointed to a column in the *Canela Record*. As was her custom, she had brought a copy to school and was perusing it for items that might interest the children. "In case there is someone in town who hasn't already heard that you and Tom were at the country club Saturday night, the *Record* announced it."

"That hardly qualifies as fame." Martha opened her lesson book, looking for today's subjects. "You know the *Record* lists everyone who attends a function. It helps circulation, since people like seeing their names in print."

"Except you."

Martha shrugged. "I know what I've done, and I don't see the need to announce it." The first class was long division, one of the most difficult subjects for Martha to teach. It was one lesson that invariably led to fidgeting students. Martha stared sightlessly out of the window, trying to find a new way to explain the concepts.

"Has Tom persuaded you to let him use your photograph?" Martha spun around. The way Anna phrased the question made her think she expected an affirmative answer.

"No, and he won't." Suddenly long division seemed like the most basic of principles, compared to making people understand why she didn't want to be the Fourth of July Woman. Martha had seen the look in Tom's eyes when she had explained her reason. His expression had reflected both sympathy and the fact that he thought her fears were irrational. Weren't all fears irrational? No matter what Tom or anyone said, Martha wouldn't take a chance with other men's lives. She had lost Henry. She couldn't, and wouldn't, be responsible for another woman enduring that kind of agony. Besides, no matter what Tom claimed, Martha's face was not one men in the trenches would dream about.

Idly, Anna turned a page of the paper. "That man could charm bees away from a honey tree. I figured he'd convince you."

"Charm has nothing to do with it."

Anna looked up, her eyes narrowing as she regarded Martha. "Does your refusal have something to do with Henry?"

"What difference would it make if it did?" Martha didn't want to lie to her friend, but there were some things that were too painful to be discussed. It was bad enough that she'd told Tom why she couldn't agree to his proposition.

Anna laid the paper down and focused her attention on Martha. The firm line of her lips told Martha she would have no chance of reviewing lesson plans until Anna had said her piece. "If your mother were alive, she would tell you what I'm going to. You need to put the past in its place, Martha. It's time to begin a new life."

What if Martha didn't want a new life? "I loved Henry." He had been one of the stable forces in her life, the boy— and then the man—she had loved for so many years. She had never envisioned a future without him, but this horrible war had changed all that.

"Of course you loved him. Everyone in Canela knows that. But Henry's not here anymore." Anna paused for a second, taking a deep breath before she spoke. "Do you think he'd want you to spend the rest of your life mourning him?"

"I don't know." Martha remembered the day they'd exchanged wedding vows, promising to love each other until death parted them. They'd been joyously happy and so in love that day, never dreaming that their final parting was imminent. The happily ever after that she and Henry had thought would endure for fifty or sixty years had lasted only a few months.

"Henry was a practical man," Anna said, her voice as confident as if she were announcing a fact that every schoolchild should know. "He loved you, and he would want you to be happy."

"I am happy."

"Are you?" This time, Anna did not bother to hide her skepticism.

Of course Martha was happy, as happy as anyone could be during wartime. When she had first received the news that Henry had been killed, she would waken in the middle of the night, crying from the pain. But now . . . Now there were days when she barely thought of him, and recently she had had difficulty conjuring his image when she closed her eyes. That bothered Martha more than she was willing to admit to anyone. Henry had died, but her love for him hadn't.

She stared out the window, wishing one of the children

would arrive and give her a reason for ignoring Anna's question. Her friend meant well. Martha knew that. But surely Anna realized that happiness wasn't guaranteed.

"If I were twenty years younger," Anna announced in her typically firm fashion, "I'd make sure that if that man left town, I was by his side."

Martha wasn't sure which image disturbed her more: the thought of Tom leaving or the picture of herself at his side.

Tom hadn't changed. Martha knew that. He was just as handsome as ever, his smile as engaging as ever. It was she who was different. Though she had tried her best, she had been unable to forget Anna's assertion that Henry would have wanted her to be happy. While Anna hadn't actually pronounced the words, her expression had left no doubt that she believed Martha's happiness was tied to Tom Fleming. First little May Gibson, then Miss Bloom, now Anna. There appeared to be an epidemic of people in Canela coupling Martha's name with Tom's.

"Did you hear from your editor?" Martha asked as they turned onto Oak. Tom had brought the car today, since some of the places on Martha's list were on opposite sides of the town. She leaned toward Tom, enunciating her question about Sidney carefully. Sidney was a neutral subject, a safe one. Martha would think about Tom's photographs, not about the way memories of his smile had intruded throughout the day, nor the way she had imagined herself walking toward him down the church aisle.

It was ridiculous, thinking of Tom Fleming, even more ridiculous thinking of him and marriage. Martha took a deep breath. It wasn't as though they had any future together. Tom wasn't a marrying man, and even if he were, he wasn't a man who'd stay in a town like Canela. As if that wasn't enough, Martha wasn't a woman who'd consider remarrying, and even if she were, it wouldn't be to a

man who couldn't live in the town that she would never
leave.

The fact that Tom's eyes sparkled assured Martha that
he was unaware of her inner turmoil. That was good. "I
was going to send Sidney a telegram, but I decided it might
be harder for him to refuse if I talked to him, so I telephoned." Tom chuckled. "It took almost as long to get the
call through as it would have to have sent a telegram and
waited for the response, but it was worth it. Even though
Sidney didn't agree, he didn't refuse, either. He said it
would all depend on the pictures."

"Will you send him the ones you've already taken?"
They were so good that Martha couldn't imagine Tom's
editor not liking them.

Tom shook his head and paused when they reached the
corner of Broad Street. "Not yet. I need a few more so that
I have pieces of the whole story." He pulled Martha's list
from his pocket and studied it for a moment. "These are
all good suggestions, and I'll use them. Right now I need
something different. Is there a new baby in town?"

A baby. She hadn't thought of that. "Bertha Wilson's
daughter is two months old."

"Do you think she'd agree to let me take their photograph?"

"I can't imagine her refusing. Bertha's very proud of
Hannah and loves to show her off."

"What about the baby's father? Is he a soldier?"

Martha nodded, thinking of the young man who had yet
to see his daughter. "Paul enlisted the same day as Theo.
Luckily for him, they were assigned to different battalions."
Instead of having Tom turn left onto Broad toward the center of town, Martha gestured right. "Bertha lives on Elm."
Five minutes later, she was knocking on the front door of
the Wilson house.

"Martha, what a surprise!" Though Bertha Wilson's

words were directed toward Martha, her smile was for Tom. "You must be the photographer everyone's talking about."

"Guilty as charged, Mrs. Wilson. I know what I'm asking is an imposition, but . . ." Perhaps Anna was right, and Tom could charm bees away from honey. Though Bertha protested that she needed to change into a prettier dress and restyle her hair, somehow Tom convinced her not only that she would be serving her country if she allowed him to take her photograph but also that she was perfect as she was. Within minutes, he had posed Bertha and her baby on the porch, standing in front of Hannah's father's blue star.

"Would you like a photograph to send to your husband?" Tom asked when he had finished taking the pictures. "Perhaps one of you rocking the baby." He gestured toward a comfortable-looking rocking chair at the other end of the porch. While the young mother's face lit with pleasure, Martha tried to control her fears.

"Paul has asked for a photograph of the baby and me," Bertha confided, "but since Mr. Harris isn't here anymore, there wasn't anyone to take it." She stroked her daughter's cheek. "Paul says his old picture of me is wrinkled from being carried everywhere. He'll be thrilled to have a new one—especially one with Hannah."

Martha took a deep breath. It seemed that Paul Wilson had suffered no ill effects from carrying his wife's photograph. That was good. It proved it was only hers that hadn't accomplished its mission of keeping her husband safe.

"Please, may I change my dress?" Bertha wrinkled her nose as she looked at her clothing. "I want Paul to see me in something he remembers."

Tom nodded. "Martha can hold the baby while you're inside."

While Bertha dressed and Tom reloaded his camera, Martha sat in the chair, the baby in her arms. She had held babies before. She had even held Hannah several times, but never before had the simple act of cradling a child in her arms filled Martha with such longing. Never before had she felt her heart ache at the thought that she had no child of her own. Never before had she looked at someone else's baby and seen a little boy, a boy who looked like a miniature version of Tom Fleming.

What on earth was happening to her?

What on earth was happening to him? Tom clenched the camera case so tightly that it dented his fingers. He shouldn't be doing this. He shouldn't be taking a picture of Martha, sitting there with a baby in her arms. He shouldn't be thinking of anything other than the fact that, even though he was intrigued by the idea of a rotogravure section, Sidney still wanted Tom's Fourth of July Woman. Sidney had been adamant about that, declaring he wouldn't buy the rotogravure feature unless Tom produced the Fourth of July Woman's photograph. But Tom was an optimist, or at least he had been until he'd crossed the Canela town limits, and so he told himself that Sidney would be so enthralled with the pictures of this quintessential village that he'd forgive the absence of one special woman's photograph. Right now, Tom could think of little besides just how beautiful that woman was and how natural it seemed for her to be cradling a baby.

"I haven't seen Canela's cemetery," Tom said to Martha half an hour later when he had taken the last picture of Bertha Wilson and they had headed back toward the center of town. "I assume there is one."

Martha's smile faltered. "Of course, there's one, but you don't need any pictures of it."

She was wrong. Tom had realized that as he'd taken the pictures of Bertha and her baby. "I want to portray the full cycle, everything in Canela from birth to death."

The blood drained from Martha's face. "I'll tell you where it is, but I'd rather not go there with you."

Tom thought he understood the reason. "Because

Henry's buried there." Undoubtedly her pilgrimages to Henry's gravesite were so personal that she didn't want anyone to witness them.

Martha shook her head. "Henry's grave is in some town in France whose name I can't pronounce. There's nothing of him here."

Tom wished he had not opened this particular subject, since it was distressing Martha. He should have remembered that the Army rarely shipped coffins back home. It was one of the things that made this war so difficult on the survivors. Perhaps it was the absence rather than the presence of a grave that made her avoid the cemetery. "I've heard that many families erect memorials for their soldiers. You and Henry's parents might find comfort in that."

Martha shook her head again. "The Yorks aren't here anymore. They left Canela a month after Henry was killed and went to Canada to be with the rest of the family."

Tom started to point out that Martha was part of their family, too, then clamped his teeth together. "That must have been difficult for you," he said as calmly as he could, though he could not understand the elder Yorks' deserting their daughter-in-law. "You had no one who understood your grief."

The urge to gather Martha into his arms and hold her close was so strong that Tom clenched his fists. He couldn't do that, not here on the street where anyone could see them. She wouldn't welcome it. Tom knew that. But, oh, how he wished he could banish the sorrow from Martha's eyes. How he wished he could make her eyes light the way they had when she had held baby Hannah. How he wished that she were holding their baby.

Martha had managed to regain her composure by the time she reached her house. It was ridiculous that she had reacted the way she had, but there had been something in Tom's expression that had made her face flush beet red.

She knew she'd been pale. The thought of the cemetery always saddened her, reminding her of loved ones she would not see again. Tom had nodded, as if he understood how she felt, and then his expression had changed. There had been such warmth in his eyes that Martha found herself thinking not of cemeteries but of babies and how wonderful it had felt to hold Hannah and how—just for an instant—she had wished the child she cradled was hers and Tom's.

It was ridiculous, just as ridiculous as the longing to be held in his arms. Fortunately, other than the traitorous blush, she had done nothing to embarrass either Tom or herself. Fortunately, though Tom Fleming was a talented man, he could not read her mind. And now that she was home, Martha could put that foolishness behind her. She would spend the evening refurbishing the costumes for the school play. That was an infallible cure for silly thoughts.

But when she opened the door, Martha discovered that she had a visitor.

"Anna, what's wrong?" Though they were friends, Anna had never come to Martha's house without an invitation. Martha hurried into the kitchen, where the older woman was seated, her slumped shoulders telling Martha this was no casual visit. "What's wrong?" Martha repeated, her alarm increasing when she saw Anna's face. Her friend's normally ruddy color had faded, leaving her ghostly white.

Anna thrust the *Canela Record* at Martha. "Look at that." Anna's finger jabbed at one column as if it were an insect that she wanted to kill.

Quickly Martha scanned the section that had distressed her friend. It was a letter to the editor, so filled with vitriol that Martha was surprised the typically moderate editor had printed it. The words were harsh, the theme even more disturbing, for the letter's author insisted that there was only one way to end the war and that was to ship "those dastardly, defiant, and dangerous Germans" back to their homeland, leaving America safe for Americans. The diatribe ended with the assertion that if deportation didn't work, the country should consider more permanent solutions.

Anna shuddered. "Kurt and I thought we would be free when we came here. And now . . ."

Martha slid her arm around Anna's shoulders, trying to reassure the older woman. "It's only one person," she said. "One crazy person who didn't have the courage to sign his name."

Anna shook her head, obviously not accepting Martha's reasoning. "What if others feel the same? What if he's speaking for many?"

That was the question Tom had asked. Martha knew that anti-German sentiment was rampant in many parts of the country, but not here. Surely not in Canela. "Don't worry, Anna. Everyone in Canela knows you're as much an American as I am."

Chapter Seven

T om was still frowning when he reached the Bradleys'
house. It was ridiculous to feel that way about Martha. Totally ridiculous. He parked the Model T, then grabbed his
camera and walked toward the front door. For Pete's sake,
he was thirty years old, and never once in that time had he
considered marriage and children. Oh, it was true that his
mother had told him on more occasions than he chose to
remember that Tom would change his mind once he met
the right woman. Mothers always said things like that.
What they didn't seem to realize was that saying something
didn't make it happen, particularly to men like Tom.

Fathers weren't immune to the wishful thinking syn-
drome, either. Hadn't his predicted that Tom would grow
tired of traveling, that the wanderlust, as he called it, would
fade? Dad had been just as wrong as Mother. His parents
loved him—Tom had never doubted that—but they didn't
understand that he had no intention of settling down or
marrying. Marriage and babies! What a crazy idea!

Tom opened the front door, continuing to walk toward
his room as he greeted Mrs. Bradley. Experience had taught
him that if he paused even to comment on the delicious
aromas wafting from the kitchen, she would spend half an

hour quizzing him about his day's activities. Today, more than most days, Tom did not want to undergo an inquisition, especially when his thoughts had detoured into dangerous territory.

Marriage! At the risk of sounding like Ebenezer Scrooge, Tom wanted to shout, "Bah, humbug." As for babies, they were a foreign species. Tom's travels had brought him into contact with many foreign species and had taught him that they fell into two categories: those whose acquaintance he enjoyed and those he should avoid at all costs. Babies fell into the second category. It was true that Martha's face had taken on a special kind of beauty, one that Tom could only describe as ethereal, when she had rocked Hannah. Martha was obviously a woman who was meant to marry and have babies. As for Tom . . . He wasn't going to think about marriage and babies. No, sirree. He was going to develop his film and hope that the photographs were as good as he thought they were.

Tom closed the door to his room firmly behind him and laid the camera on the old table. As soon as supper was over, he would develop today's pictures so that he could deliver Bertha Wilson's photographs tomorrow morning. He would give her the ones he had taken for her husband and would show her the ones that he was considering using for the rotogravure. What he wouldn't show Bertha or anyone else were the photographs he had taken of Martha holding the baby and looking as beautiful as a Madonna. Tom frowned. He was a fool to have taken those pictures. If he kept them, they would be one more reminder of thoughts he didn't want to entertain.

Think of something else, Tom admonished himself.

The Canela cemetery had been a pleasant surprise. He had feared that he would find it depressing. Instead, from the moment he had opened the iron gates and entered the tree-shaded plot, Tom had felt a sense of peace. Canela was living up to its slogan of being The Friendliest Little Town in East Texas. Even its graveyard was friendly. Though the majority of the markers were simple granite tombstones, the cemetery boasted a number of interesting monuments. As he wandered along the dirt paths, Tom's eye had been drawn to a white stone dove perched on top of a tombstone. A few other markers had angels or crosses; this was the only one with a bird. Intrigued, Tom approached the monument. When he read the inscription, he nodded. It wasn't simply that he recognized the verse from Psalms as one his mother had chosen for her own mother's grave. *Oh that I had wings like a dove, for then would I fly away and be at rest* wasn't, Tom suspected, an unusual selection for a gravestone. What caused him to nod with satisfaction was the sense of rightness. It wasn't coincidence that this was the monument that had first caught his eye, nor was it co-incidence that the tombstone belonged to Paul Wilson's grandfather. This was the monument Tom would use.

While another photographer might have ended his set of pictures with the cemetery, Tom decided that he would be-gin the rotogravure section with the first Wilson's grave and end it with a photograph of Bertha Wilson holding Hannah. Surely then readers would understand that nothing, not even this horrible war, could disturb the circle of life. That was a positive thought. It was the theme Tom wanted to convey with his pictures.

He had his theme. He had taken the majority of the pho-tographs. That's what he ought to be thinking about, not the memory of Martha holding a baby in her arms nor that absurd wish that the baby had been his. Tom didn't want a baby. Of course he didn't. And that made it all the more annoying that he couldn't banish the image from his mind.

He pulled out his watch and flicked it open. Fifteen minutes before Hank Bradley normally arrived home, twenty minutes before Linda Bradley would serve supper. Tom would spend that time sorting the photographs he'd already taken, choosing the ones he was still considering for the rotogravure. He spread the pictures on the table, and as he did, he frowned. Seconds later, his frown turned to a scowl.

"Mrs. Bradley." Tom tried to keep from bellowing as he entered the kitchen. His landlady was standing in front of the stove, stirring a pot of what smelled like vegetable stew.

"Yes, Tom." She turned and smiled, but his expression made that smile fade. "Is something wrong?"

Tom took a deep breath, reminding himself that anger solved nothing. "My pictures seem out of order," he said as calmly as he could. "I thought we had agreed that you would not disturb anything on the table."

His landlady appeared perplexed. "I didn't touch anything. I don't even dust the table when I clean the rest of your room." Tom couldn't argue with that statement, for there was normally a thin coating of dust on the table. That did not, however, explain why his photographs had been reordered as if someone had looked through them. Tom told himself that that wasn't a crime. A photographer wanted people to look at his pictures. It was simply that he wasn't ready for these photographs to be seen. Knowing that someone had rifled through them made him feel as if something precious had been taken from him.

Linda Bradley pursed her lips, obviously considering the problem. "It must be that the wind blew them," she said. "It's been so warm that I've opened the window a couple times. That's what happened."

Though Tom doubted the wind had been responsible, there was little he could say in face of Mrs. Bradley's staunch assertion. The problem would disappear, he reminded himself, when he left Canela. Oddly, that thought provided no consolation.

Martha dipped her pen into the inkwell as she considered how to begin the letter to her sister.

Dear Carolyn,

Something rather disturbing happened today. The Record *published an anonymous letter claiming that all German-Americans should be driven out of town. The author didn't suggest tar and feathers, but he wasn't far from that. What bothers me, Carolyn, is not knowing who is filled with so much hatred. I would have suspected Hank Bradley. Ever since his son was drafted he's been outspoken in his dislike for all things German. The problem is, the letter was very well written. The author even used alliteration. I'm sure I don't need to remind you that Mr. Bradley is not our most highly educated resident. And that, Carolyn, is what worries me. I can't believe there are two people in Canela who are so bigoted. Don't they understand that the real enemy is on the other side of the ocean?*

As she wrote the final words, Martha shook her head. She couldn't send Carolyn a letter like this. Her sister was in France, helping to heal men who had lived in trenches and who had been wounded in battle. A letter to the *Canela Record* was trivial compared to the tragedies Carolyn faced each day. Martha crumpled the page and pulled out another sheet.

Dear Carolyn,

Do you remember my telling you that a famous photographer came to Canela? He's probably as well-known as that journalist Emily said she had met. Yes, Carolyn, I'm referring to the man who seems to have sent our normally practical little sister into a tizzy. Tom—that's the photographer's name, Tom Fleming— is taking pictures of Canela. If his editor agrees, our town will be famous. People all over the country will see how beautiful our hometown is. The Gainey Gazette *is distributed to our men in the trenches. Can you imagine Theo's surprise when he sees pictures of Canela?*

Before the ink had a chance to dry, Martha tossed the sheet into the wastebasket. There was no point in reminding Carolyn of their brother. She had been the first of them to hear what had happened to Theo's brigade, and the news had devastated her. Martha stared out the window, trying to find something to tell her sister. Finally she picked up her pen again.

Dear Carolyn,
*   It sounds as though you're cap-over-boots in love with a very special man. I wish I were there to hug you and wish you both well. If Emily were with you, she'd nod and tell you that he's your silver lining. You've had your share of dark clouds, especially recently. Take Emily's advice and mine and enjoy every minute of your time together.*

Because, Martha thought as she sealed the envelope, no one knew how long that time would be.

It was a beautiful day. Martha hummed softly as she wrapped the crock of beans in a newspaper. How many times had she seen her mother do exactly the same thing with the same crock, telling her daughters that this was the best way to keep food warm? Carolyn and Emily had laughed when they'd learned that Martha had kept the crock. They had pointed out that this one was chipped and that she could buy a bigger, better one from Mr. Martin. That was true. What Martha's sisters didn't understand was the sentimental value that she placed on this battered piece of pottery or the satisfaction she found in keeping traditions alive.

Glancing out the window again, Martha smiled. Today

she was going to share one of her traditions with Tom, and it appeared to be the perfect day for it. Today was the day she planned to show Tom the bluebonnets that made this part of Texas so beautiful each spring. Bluebonnets were pretty even on a gray day, but when the sun was shining and the sky unbroken by clouds, they were nothing less than spectacular. This was what she wanted Tom to see.

Martha folded the tablecloth and placed it in the basket. The week had gone quickly. Fortunately, there had been no more virulent letters to the editor, and Anna seemed to have regained her equilibrium. Just as fortunately, Martha had had no more awkward moments with Tom. It was true that she couldn't stop herself from dreaming of him, but at least while they were together, she hadn't blushed every single time he looked at her.

When she heard the unmistakable sound of Tom's Model T, Martha slipped on her gloves and walked outside. The smile that Tom gave her made her glad she had worn this dress. Though it was a simple muslin frock, her sisters had told her that the deep navy color highlighted her hair and eyes.

Tom was dressed more casually than Martha had ever seen him, with a straw boater set at a jaunty angle. It was early in the year to be wearing a straw hat—tradition said that the straw season was June, July, and August—but Martha suspected that the unseasonably warm weather had caused Tom to break with tradition. There was no doubt about it: straw hats were cooler than felt. There was also no doubt that Tom was less tied to tradition than she was.

Tom's gaze moved from Martha to the object she held in her right hand. "Is that a picnic basket?"

She nodded. "I know you like to take pictures in different lights, and I didn't want you to have to rush back simply because it was mealtime."

Tom took the basket from her and placed it in the car. "You're a mind reader," he said as he opened the door for

Martha. "I had wondered where we'd be able to find lunch."

There was no such thing as a mind reader, Martha told herself. She couldn't read his, and she certainly hoped Tom could not read hers. It would be embarrassing to have him know how handsome she found him and how often she dreamed of him. Even worse, she would be mortified if he knew just what she dreamed—how in her dreams, he held her in his arms and kissed her. No, Martha couldn't possibly let him know that!

"It's nothing fancy," she said, dismissing the effort she had put into planning their picnic, "but at least we won't starve."

He started the car and headed west on Chestnut. When they reached the edge of Canela, Tom turned to Martha. "Won't the townspeople gossip if we're gone for several hours?"

She shrugged. "By now you should know that everything you do feeds the rumor mill here. You're the most exciting thing that has happened to this town in many years." And the most exciting thing that had happened to Martha, though she had no intention of telling him that. "If I were unmarried, going for a drive without a chaperone would be scandalous. Fortunately, I have a bit more freedom as a widow." It was, Martha reflected, the first time she had found anything positive about widowhood.

They drove for several hours, stopping occasionally so that Tom could take photographs. Though Martha had imagined that he would try to capture the beauty of the countryside, he focused on individual flowers, the scarlet Indian paintbrush whose tips looked as if they'd been dipped in paint; the red, orange, and yellow firewheel that turned the ground into a brilliantly colored tapestry; and her favorite, the bluebonnets. Each time they would stop, Tom would set up the tripod and carefully compose a picture, frequently moving from one spot to another until he was satisfied that he had the best view. While he was work-ing, Martha said nothing, simply watched him, marveling at the concentration that he put into each picture. But when they were back in the car, they would talk. Their conver-sation wasn't earthshaking, and yet Martha found the casual camaraderie comforting. It felt right being here with Tom.

"Is this what you do when you travel?" she asked, won-dering how long it had taken him to drive to Canela if he stopped so often to take photographs.

"Sometimes. I rarely have a guide, though, so finding the right spot to photograph is often a matter of luck."

They drove for a few more minutes, and as they did, Martha felt a sense of anticipation mingled with apprehen-sion. She knew what was around the next bend, and it never failed to thrill her. But Tom was with her, and that changed everything. What if he didn't like the place she was taking him? It shouldn't matter. Nothing horrible would happen if he found her special place ordinary. Martha knew that, and still she worried. She couldn't explain why, but it seemed important that Tom appreciate this place that had been such a special part of her childhood.

She directed him to turn left, then right again. Martha held her breath as they approached a field that was so filled with bluebonnets that the ground looked as if it were cov-ered with a blue carpet. A weathered gray windmill stood in one corner of the field, while the deep green of mesquite bushes formed a border at the far end. Would he like it?

"What a beautiful place!" Tom slowed, then stopped the car and reached for his camera. "Do you mind?"

Martha shook her head as relief coursed through her. She and Tom might not agree on everything, but they both found beauty in the same things.

When he had taken several pictures, Tom looked at the sky, apparently assessing the sun's position. "Would this be a good place to have our picnic?"

It was what she had planned. "If you're hungry."

Tom simply laughed and patted his stomach. "I can always eat. Surely you've learned that by now." He retrieved the basket from the back of the car and walked next to her as she led the way. When they reached a spot where the mesquite provided a bit of shade, he helped her spread the tablecloth on the ground.

"How did you discover this place?" he asked, placing the picnic basket on one corner of the cloth.

Martha arranged her skirts as she sat on the other end of the cloth. "I can't take credit for it. My parents used to bring us here each year when the bluebonnets were in bloom. Carolyn and I would pick flowers and try to braid them, while Emily and Theo would challenge each other to a race." Martha smiled, remembering the time Theo had tried to climb a mesquite, only to discover that the limbs would not support him. It had been a day like this, with a few puffy clouds scudding across the sky. Though he had had the breath knocked out of him, Theo had laughed. Only Emily had appeared frightened at the thought of harm befalling her twin.

"What about your parents?" Tom was only a foot away from Martha. He'd positioned himself so that his good ear was turned toward her, and though his posture seemed relaxed, he appeared to be studying her. Martha felt the color begin to rise to her cheeks. Even without trying, this man wreaked havoc with her common sense. He had only to fix those beautiful blue eyes on her and she blushed like a schoolgirl.

Tom leaned forward, propping his hands on his knees. "What were your parents doing while the four of you played?"

"After we ate, they'd sit here and watch us, and when they thought we weren't looking, they'd kiss." *Oh, no!* What a silly thing to say. The instant the words were out of her mouth, Martha wished she could retract them. She didn't want to think about kisses, particularly with Tom sitting so close that she could smell the faintly astringent scent of his shaving cream, particularly after the way she dreamed of him each night and the way each of those dreams ended with him enfolding her in his arms and pressing his lips to hers.

"That sounds like fun." The hint of laughter in Tom's voice made Martha wonder whether he sensed her confusion. Surely not. Surely he thought her heightened color was caused by the sun.

"Picking flowers was fun," she agreed, "even though Carolyn and I weren't good at the braiding part."

"If you ask me, I think it was your parents who had the fun."

The way he stared at her lips made Martha's blush deepen. "Oh, Tom!" What was wrong with her that she spent half her time as red as an apple?

"I won't believe you if you tell me you've never been kissed."

A cloud slid across the sun, and for a second Tom's face was shadowed. Martha didn't need sunlight to tell her he was teasing her. "Of course I've been kissed, but not here." She and Henry had never come to this spot.

"My mother always said there's no time like the present." And before Martha could protest, Tom had closed the distance between them and drawn her into his arms.

She had dreamed of Tom. She had dreamed of being held in his arms. She had dreamed of his kiss and how sweet it would be. Reality, Martha soon realized, was far better than dreams. Though she had a vivid imagination, that imagination had not come close to the reality of Tom's embrace. It was warm and sweet and better than anything she'd experienced. Nothing in her life had ever felt as wonderful as having Tom's lips on hers, of feeling his arms around her. It was a moment of sheer perfection. If only it would never end!

* * *

If only he didn't have to end it! Though it was one of the most difficult things he'd ever done, Tom dragged his lips away from Martha's. He hadn't wanted to end the kiss. No, indeed. He had wanted that kiss to go on forever and ever, and that had scared him. It wasn't the first time Tom had kissed a woman, but it was the first time he'd felt as if the world had suddenly stopped spinning on its axis, as if nothing existed but the two of them and a field of bluebonnets. It was the first time he'd felt as if nothing mattered but being with this woman and spending the rest of his life with her. And that was truly frightening. Tom wasn't ready for that kind of commitment. Not today and probably not ever.

He moved to the opposite corner of the tablecloth, wishing he dared pick up his camera and capture Martha's expression. Her face was flushed, her eyes shone, and her lips were curved in the sweetest of smiles. Tom's instincts told him it would be almost as good a picture as The Photograph. Perhaps it was best, though, that he not have this picture. There was no sense in torturing himself with memories of a moment that would never be repeated.

"If your mother's chicken smelled as good as yours," Tom said in a desperate attempt to put the world back on its axis, "I can understand why your father didn't stray too far from the picnic basket."

As if she welcomed the neutral subject, Martha made a show of sniffing. "I don't smell the chicken."

"You put it in this corner of the basket."

As Tom pointed, Martha nodded. "You're right. Your sense of smell must be keener than mine."

"Either that, or I'm hungrier."

"Did anyone ever tell you that you're not very subtle?"

Thank goodness, it was once again an ordinary day. Tom was having a picnic with a beautiful woman, and maybe— in a hundred years or so—he would be able to forget how wonderful it had felt to kiss that woman.

"If not being subtle gets me chicken and baked beans, I don't mind."

Martha opened the basket lid and started to bring out containers of food. "There's chocolate cake, too."

Before he could stop them, the stupid words flew from his mouth. "I think I'm in love."

He didn't mean anything by it, just as he hadn't meant anything by the kiss. Martha knew that. She also knew that it was silly to feel flustered simply because a man had kissed her and said he was in love. It wasn't as though Tom had been serious about either one of them. The chocolate cake had precipitated the declaration, which only proved that he'd been joking about love. As for the kiss, Tom knew Martha was a person who believed in carrying on traditions, and when she had told him how her parents had kissed when they had picnicked here, he'd wanted her to share that tradition. That was the only reason Tom had kissed her. It wasn't because he cared about her, and it most definitely wasn't because he was in love with her. Men, with the notable exception of Henry, didn't fall in love with Martha Wentworth.

It was a beautiful day, the perfect day for a picnic. Even the clouds that were scudding across the sky couldn't mar that. Martha took a deep breath and reached for the jug of iced tea. She would enjoy the sun and the bluebonnets and do her best to forget how it had felt to be held in Tom's arms. She wouldn't think about how much she had enjoyed his kiss. And she most definitely wouldn't let her mind repeat the words he'd said.

Somehow, though she was not sure how, Martha managed to pretend that nothing unusual had happened. She set out the food and, to her surprise, found that she could swallow fried chicken and beans. It was true that she and Tom sat on opposite sides of the tablecloth and that she had placed containers of food between them. That helped. Even though the distance was only a few feet, at least there was no danger of their hands touching. That was good. While they ate, she and Tom talked about the school play, how the town would enjoy the Fourth of July carousel and which photographs Tom should include in his proposal for the rotogravure. They did not talk about kisses or love or anything foolish like that. That was very good. Of course it was.

Martha was so intent on keeping her mind away from dangerous subjects that she paid no attention to the sky and to the large black cloud that suddenly covered the sun. A second later, a bolt of lightning was followed by a loud clap of thunder. Instantly, the cloud opened, drenching Tom and Martha and the field of bluebonnets.

As she struggled to her feet and began to throw the dishes into the basket, Tom laughed.

"Do I look that funny?" Martha demanded, wadding the tablecloth and tossing it on top of the now sodden newspaper. Her hat was ruined, her dress soaking wet.

"You look beautiful, Martha." Tom took the basket from her and started sprinting toward the car. "Nothing can change that."

It wasn't the first time he had told her she was beautiful, but it was the first time Tom—or anyone—had told her she was beautiful when water squished in her shoes, her skirts were soaked and her hair clung wetly to her cheeks. The thought was so absurd that Martha almost laughed herself.

"Why were you laughing?" she asked again when they were inside the car, protected from the rain that was now streaming across the road.

Rivulets of water dripped from Tom's hat. Impatiently, he removed it and let the remaining moisture drain onto the floor. "It was the thunder," he said. "I always laugh at it."

Martha felt her eyes widen in amazement. "I never thought there was anything amusing about thunder." The neighbors' dog had cowered under a bed when it thundered, and there had been times when Martha had been tempted to follow suit. Never once had she considered laughing, but Tom did. Perhaps this was like her sister Carolyn's crazy idea of dancing in the rain. Perhaps it was how he coped with problems.

"It started when I was seven," Tom said, as if that explained everything. "That's when I caught a fever that wouldn't go away. My parents told me that I was delirious for several days, and they were afraid that I would die. When the fever finally subsided, I was still alive, but I couldn't hear a thing."

"Oh, Tom." Martha laid a hand on his, wanting to comfort the small boy he'd once been. Rain continued to beat on the car roof. Martha tried but failed to imagine what it must have been like to see rain but not hear it, to see a dog open its mouth but hear no bark.

"It was the most frightening thing that has ever happened to me." Tom's eyes darkened with remembered pain. "I didn't know what to do. I could talk, but I wasn't sure anyone understood me, because most of the time, no one responded. Afterwards, my parents told me I was whispering so softly that they couldn't hear me. All that time I was convinced I was shouting."

Martha shuddered as she thought of how terrified the young Tom must have been.

"I couldn't hear them, and I couldn't read lips. There I was, trapped in a silent world."

Tears welled in her eyes as Martha squeezed Tom's hand. "I can't even imagine how awful that must have been."

"I was sure I'd never hear again, and I didn't know what to do." Tom threaded his fingers through hers, and the warmth of his hand began to comfort her. Martha blinked. She had wanted to help Tom, but it seemed that he was the one providing comfort. "About a month went by, and then we had a violent rainstorm." Tom continued the story. "There was lots of lightning. My parents claim there was also a lot of thunder, but I can't tell you whether that's true or not. All I know is, as the storm got closer, one clap of thunder was louder than the rest. It was so loud that I heard it." Tom's eyes darkened again with the memory. "When I heard it, I laughed from sheer joy. I could hear *something*. After a month of silence, it felt like a miracle to me." Tom looked through the windscreen at the sky that was even now lightening, then smiled as he turned back toward Martha. "Eventually most of my hearing returned in the one ear, but to this day, whenever it thunders, I laugh."

"It's a lovely story," Martha said. "I'm a little confused, though. I understand why you laughed that day, but I don't understand why you continue laughing at the thunder."

Tom's expression was serious as his eyes met Martha's. "Thunder reminds me that no matter how bad things seem, something good will come from them, if you only look for it." He gestured toward the rain that had puddled in the road. "There was so much rain that day that my parents were worried about flooding. They were bemoaning the fact that rain always came at the wrong time, but when I regained some hearing, no one minded the water in the cellar. The rain had brought back my hearing."

Martha nodded. "You sound like my sister Emily. She always tries to find silver linings in clouds. I don't know how she does it, but she can find something positive in even the bleakest of situations. In fact, when *Pollyanna* was first published, I was certain it was based on her."

"I'm not a Pollyanna," Tom was quick to say, "but I do believe there's good to be found in everything. Even being deaf. I'm convinced that being hard of hearing forced me to develop my other senses." Tom's eyes were serious as he looked at her. "I've been told that I see things differently from other people, and that that's why I became a photographer. That may be true." Tom's smile was wry. "I would never have chosen to be deaf, but if I had to be, I'm thankful that something good came from it."

Martha closed her eyes for a second, wishing she could share Tom's optimism. In her experience, silver linings and happy endings were meant for other people.

Chapter Eight

Martha wrote the last of the day's assignments on the board, then laid the chalk aside. Where was Anna? Normally the woman was as punctual as the German trains were reputed to be, arriving at exactly the same time each morning. Today she was late, and that was so unusual that it worried Martha. Had something happened to Anna? Had she fallen and hurt herself? Had she spilled coffee and burned her hand? Martha shuddered as she considered the possibilities, then relaxed when she heard her assistant's footsteps. Her relief lasted only a second. Anna, normally unflappable Anna, had been crying. Her nose was red, her face blotched with tears.

"What's wrong?"

Anna stood in the doorway, as if she were afraid to enter the schoolroom where she normally spent the day. She opened her mouth, then closed it again. *"Schrecklich,"* she said at last.

Even more than Anna's tear-stained face, her use of her native language alarmed Martha. It was only in moments of extreme happiness or sorrow that Anna slipped into German. "What is terrible?" Martha crossed the room and gently propelled her assistant into a chair. Anna's whole

117

body was trembling, and she moved with the slow, awkward gait of a much older person. She sat with her hands clasped, her knuckles whitened by the grip. "They refused ... They wouldn't let ... They called me ... the enemy." Whatever had happened was so traumatic that Anna could not complete the sentences.

Martha thought for a second, trying to imagine what could have upset her friend. Then she remembered that Anna had planned to visit the bank before she came to school this morning.

"Did someone refuse to sell you a Liberty Bond?" she asked.

"Ja." Anna nodded, and tears welled in her eyes. "They said the bonds were only for *real* Americans." Covering her face with her hands, Anna began to sob.

Anger rushed through Martha with the speed and ferocity of a summer fire sweeping across a sun-dried field. How dare anyone hurt Anna! What kind of person could say such horrible things? This was worse than the letter to the editor of the *Record*. That had been anonymous, directed at all Germans, not only Anna. This was personal. Just as bad, it had occurred at the bank that had been part of Martha's family for generations.

Martha's first instinct was to race to the bank and demand that whoever was in charge of Liberty Bonds retract his words and sell one to Anna. But that, she knew, would accomplish little. The damage had already been done. Almost as quickly as it had flared, Martha's anger subsided, replaced by sorrow that Anna was suffering. Martha's heart went out to her friend. There had to be something she could do to help her. Words had inflicted the wounds; perhaps words would heal them. "You're a real American," Martha said. "Just because you weren't born in Texas doesn't make you any less of an American than me." Martha believed that with every fiber of her being. Didn't she spend days teaching the students that what made America such a great country was its people, that the blending of different cultures created a country that was strong and vibrant?

Anna shook her head slowly, unconvinced by Martha's argument.

"You're a real American, Anna. Maybe more real than I am, because you chose to make this your country. For the rest of us, it was an accident of birth."

Tears continued to stream down Anna's face. "They hate me. They told me I wasn't welcome here and that I shouldn't be allowed near the children." Anna's voice broke as she pronounced the last words. This, Martha knew, was the most devastating of the blows her friend had been dealt, for Anna loved working with the children. She had told Martha that the hours she spent in the classroom had helped her through the difficult months after her husband's death. And now her work brought meaning to her days. If she didn't come to school, Anna's life would have a great void.

"I'm the teacher," Martha said firmly. "I decide who helps me."

But Anna shook her head, this time so violently that one of her braids threatened to come loose from the coronet. "These people are dangerous. I've seen their kind before." Her eyes darkened with the memory. "They're why Kurt and I left Germany."

Though Anna had not shared the details of her life in Germany, Martha had heard that political repression had been one of the reasons Anna and her husband had come to America.

"We'll ignore them."

"That doesn't work." Anna spoke with the voice of experience. "I'm sorry, Martha, but I can't help you any longer. It wouldn't be safe."

Nothing Martha said was able to persuade her friend differently, and before the first of the pupils arrived, Anna had left. Martha's heart ached as she watched her friend walk away, her shoulders slumped, her gait faltering. Anna, Martha guessed, was crying, just as she was. Briskly, Martha dashed the tears from her cheeks. She wouldn't upset the children. When they asked where Anna was, Martha simply told them Mrs. Gottlieb wasn't feeling well and might not be able to come to school for the next few days. Surely by then Anna would realize that her place was here with the students.

"Where's Anna?" Tom asked when he met Martha at the end of the day.

"Didn't Mr. Martin tell you?" Martha knew that Tom spent most mornings with the shopkeeper, and Mr. Martin prided himself on being the first to know whatever was happening in Canela. When Tom shook his head, Martha felt a bit of the tension drain from her body. If Mr. Martin hadn't heard the story, perhaps Anna's humiliation hadn't been as public as Martha feared.

"I don't know what to do to convince her she's wrong," Martha told Tom as she concluded the explanation. "In my heart, I know that the best thing is for Anna to pretend nothing happened. We can't let the bullies win."

Though Tom nodded as if he agreed with her, his face was solemn. "My impression is that Anna is stubborn. Once she makes up her mind, nothing will change it."

"I wish I could disagree with you, but that's Anna, all right." As they crossed the street, Martha turned to Tom. "I know it's selfish of me, but I can't help wondering how I'm going to get through the school play without her. Anna's always been the one who kept order."

"Can I help you? I'm not Anna, but there must be something I can do."

Martha raised an eyebrow. Tom had made no secret of his discomfort around the students. "You're volunteering to spend the longest two hours of your life with thirty overly excited children?"

"I was going to be there anyway to take pictures. How difficult can it be?"

"You'll find out."

To Martha's surprise, the play was more successful than she had dared hope. The children, though obviously nervous over the prospect of performing for their parents, were better behaved than in previous years. Martha suspected it was because they were in awe of Tom and more than a little afraid of his camera. Knowing that someone might capture the act on film seemed to deter the normal pranks.

"Congratulations," Tom said when the last of the parents and children had left and Martha had started to return the schoolroom to normality. Though the play had been held outdoors so that they could accommodate the audience, the children had changed into their costumes inside, and in doing so, they had managed to overturn several desks and strew books on the floor. "Everyone said this was the best play ever."

Martha chuckled. "They say that every year, but it did go well—thanks to you."

When he had moved the desks back into neat rows, Tom looked at Martha. "You wish Anna had been here." It was a statement, not a question.

"I kept hoping I'd see her in the audience." Martha had visited Anna every day, trying to convince her to return to school. When her pleas had been to no avail, she had suggested that Anna attend the performance, arguing that the children would enjoy having her watch them. Though Anna had shaken her head, Martha had not given up hope until the very end. "Anna has done so much for this town that I hate to see anyone hurt her."

Tom straightened the last desk. "One of the things I've learned is that you can't solve every problem."

Martha knew that, but she also knew how important it was to fight for what was right. "I want to solve this one.

Anna's my friend, and friends help each other." She took a step closer to Tom and looked up at him, willing him to listen. It was vital that he understood how she felt. Though he had no siblings and didn't understand the ties that bound her to her sisters and brother, surely he had friends. Surely he could empathize with her.

Tom nodded slowly. "I agree with you, but I'm afraid that this is one battle you're not going to win."

She wouldn't believe that. Martha tried another tactic. "If I adopt the Tom Fleming school of philosophy, I should be able to find something positive in what happened to Anna. So far I haven't been able to. What good do you think could possibly come out of this?"

"I don't know. Sometimes it's not obvious for a long time."

"And sometimes it never happens." That was what Martha feared.

The pictures were good. Tom smiled as he held the plate up to the red light. At least one thing had gone right today. Somehow during the chaotic preparation for the play, he had managed to capture the children's enthusiasm. Though there were a number of eminently publishable photographs, the one Tom liked the best was Paul Anderson pulling May Gibson's pigtails. It was a typical childish action, but the fact that they were both in Pilgrim costumes and were attempting to look serious gave the picture a special appeal. Sidney would like it. Tom knew that instinctively. And maybe in the next town he would find someone who could be his Fourth of July Woman.

Though Tom hated the thought of settling for second best, Sidney had been adamant. Unless Tom produced the Fourth of July Woman, there would be no rotogravure section and no further work with the *Gainey Gazette*. If Tom wanted a career—and he did—he would have to pack his equipment and head for the next town.

The next town? Frowning, Tom set the plates out to dry. The thought of new places had always excited him. His parents claimed Tom was a man who enjoyed the journey as much as the destination, and he couldn't disagree. The truth was, he was not a man who liked staying in one place for more than a few days. Why, then, did the prospect of leaving Canela seem so unappealing? Tom had already been here far longer than any other place, except for major cities like Paris and London. He had taken the last of the pictures that he needed for the rotogravure. There was no reason to remain.

Except for Martha.

Tom carried the bucket of rinse water outside. There was no point in deluding himself. He cared about Martha. He enjoyed her company, and he didn't want to leave her. He might even love her. If Mr. Martin and the rest of the busybodies in Canela were right, he did love her. Tom wasn't sure about that. He wasn't sure what love was, but he knew that what he felt for Martha was different from anything he'd ever felt before. He knew that when he was with her the thought of happily ever after didn't seem impossible. He also knew that the thought of driving on to the next town without Martha held no appeal. Tom didn't want to stay in Canela. Heavens, no. Settling down in one town was not the life for him. No, sirree. But that didn't mean he had to leave Martha behind. She could go with him.

He was smiling as he returned to the house. Martha had asked him what good could possibly come from the hatred that Anna had faced. Perhaps the good was that now Martha would see her hometown as it really was. Perhaps now she'd take off those rose-colored glasses and recognize that Canela was like every other town in the country. It had good in it, but it also had bad. Once she recognized that, she'd be willing to leave. With him. They'd travel the country together, looking for perfect spots to photograph, and when it rained, they'd laugh at the thunder.

Tom's smile turned into a grin. That was the answer. That was what he wanted. Tom Fleming wanted a bride.

He was going to leave. She knew that. Martha tried to keep a smile fixed on her face as she brushed her hair. It was the day after the school play. In all probability, it was the day Tom Fleming would leave Canela. She bit her lip. It was no use trying to smile. The most she could do was keep the tears at bay. Tom had never promised that he would stay. In fact, he had been forthright from the very beginning, telling her that he would be in Canela only long enough to take the photographs he needed. That time was now over. He had no reason to remain, and so he would leave, just as everyone she loved did.

Martha's hand stopped and she stared at her reflection, watching the blood drain from her face. What on earth had caused her to think that? She didn't love Tom. Her legs suddenly unstable, she sank onto the bed. She didn't love Tom. But as she shook her head in an effort to clear her thoughts, Martha knew she was trying to delude herself. It was true. She loved Tom. Indeed she did. That was the only way she could describe how she felt about him. It wasn't the same kind of love she felt for Carolyn and Emily and Theo, and it certainly wasn't what she had felt for Henry. This was different. Very different. Never before had thoughts of a person filled so much of her life. Never before had Martha dreamed of the same person every single night. And never before had she feared the emptiness that that person's leaving would create.

She loved Tom. She wouldn't deny that, just as she wouldn't ignore the fact that they had no future together. Tom Fleming was the Peripatetic Photographer. That meant that traveling was as necessary to him as breathing. He needed it to survive, just as Martha needed the constancy of living in one place. Those were undeniable facts, just as it was a fact that Tom would soon be gone, and when he was, Martha would have to live with the loneliness.

"I plan to mail the pictures to Sidney today," Tom said as they walked toward the school. He had met her at her front gate as he did each morning. It was surely only Martha's imagination that Tom looked more handsome than normal, that his eyes seemed to sparkle more than usual and that his smile was warmer than she'd ever seen it. Could it be the thought of leaving Canela that made him look so happy? Of course it was. Hadn't she just reminded herself how important travel was to Tom?

"Then your work in Canela is done." Oh, how she hated pronouncing the words! But Martha knew better than to delude herself. Today was his last day. He would say good-bye at the schoolhouse, and she would never see him again.

Tom offered her his arm as they crossed Main Street. When they were on the other side, he turned to her. "I thought I'd stay until I heard from Sidney." They were simple words, but the happiness that swept through Martha was anything but simple. For a second she wanted to dance from sheer joy. Tom would be here for at least another week.

"Sidney might want a few more photos," Tom continued. Martha didn't care what the reason was; all that mattered was that Tom wasn't leaving today. "And maybe I can convince you to let me use you as the Fourth of July Woman."

His words dashed her happiness as effectively as a bucket of cold water. This was why Tom was staying. It wasn't because he cared about her. He hadn't mentioned using her photograph for so long that Martha thought he had given up the idea. She was obviously wrong, as wrong as she had been to attribute anything to the kiss they had shared in the bluebonnet field. She might love him, but to Tom, she was nothing more than the subject of a photograph. Oh, how that thought hurt!

"I'm sorry, Tom. You can call me superstitious if you like, but I can't agree to that."

The corner of his mouth quirked upward. "Not even to help a friend?"

"What do you mean?"

"I thought I was your friend."

"You are." As she pronounced the words, Martha felt as if one of Mr. Edison's light bulbs had just turned on, banishing the shadows from her thoughts. Her feelings were clear now. Tom was her friend, and she loved him. Of course. It made sense. The reason that love felt so different to her was that never before had Martha had a man as a friend. Theo was her brother; Henry had been her husband. And Tom . . . Tom was her friend. That was why she cared for him the way she did, why she dreamed about him, why she dreaded his leaving.

"You told me that friends help others." Though his tone was still casual, Martha felt as if he were an attorney, making a case in front of a jury.

"They do," she agreed. They had reached the schoolhouse and stood by the steps. In a minute Martha would go inside. It would be a day like so many others. No one would know that today was the day Martha York discovered she loved a friend.

"What if I told you that your photograph was the one I needed to save my career?"

She stared at him, wondering what kind of joke this was. "I would say you were the most persistent man I've ever met. You'll do anything to get your way." Including pretending that his career needed someone to save it. What a ridiculous thought! Everyone knew that Tom Fleming was one of the country's best photographers. He didn't need Martha to help him. But Tom was clever. She would be the last to deny that. He had been in Canela long enough and had spent enough time with her to recognize that she felt an obligation to help her friends, and now he was trying to exploit that.

"Does that mean you won't let me use it?"

"It does."

Chapter Nine

"So, are you sparking the gal?"

He could, Tom supposed, feign ignorance, pretending he didn't recognize the term *sparking* or that he didn't realize Mr. Martin was referring to Martha. Since he doubted the shopkeeper would believe him in either case, Tom answered with a question of his own. "Would it bother anyone if I were?"

Mr. Martin shook his head more vehemently than usual. " 'Course not. We all think the world of Martha. I reckon she's overdue for some happiness." Before Tom could interject a word, the shopkeeper continued. "I never did see a gal so in-fat-u-ate-ed." He pronounced each syllable separately, then grinned as if proud that he'd remembered the word. "The rest of us couldn't figger out what she saw in him. Henry York was a nice enough fella, but nothing special, if you know what I mean. Martha didn't see it that way. She fairly worshiped the ground he walked on."

"Saint Henry."

Mr. Martin cupped a hand around his ear as if he were the one whose hearing was impaired. "What'd you say?"

"Nothing." Tom tried not to frown. Though the shopkeeper's words came as no surprise, they reminded Tom of just how difficult his undertaking might be.

Martha wasn't certain what surprised her most, the fact that Tom stood at the foot of the stairs, an arm behind his back, or the expression she saw on his face. When they had parted that morning, she had thought she might not see him again. Though Tom had said he was planning to stay in Canela until he heard from his editor, that had been before Martha had refused to let him use her photograph. He had obviously been unhappy about her decision. The way his lips had thinned when he'd heard her reply had told her that. For an instant, Martha had thought he was going to protest, but then one of the schoolchildren had arrived, and Tom had said nothing more than good-bye. It was the tone of that word that had made Martha fear he'd leave Canela that morning. But he hadn't. Instead, he was here, waiting for her as he did every day, but looking very different. Martha had seen him angry, happy, sad, even bored. Never before had she seen him looking sheepish.

"Is something wrong?" Could Tom's expression be caused by regret that he had tried to persuade her to be his Fourth of July Woman?

His lips quirked upward. "I hope not." Slowly, Tom drew his arm from behind his back and held out a circlet of flowers. "When I saw that blue dress this morning," he said, nodding at the simple cotton frock she was wearing, "I thought you might like this. It's for your hair," he added.

Martha stared at the bluebonnets, wondering if she had misjudged Tom. Perhaps he did care about her, at least a little. Perhaps he did see her as something more than a woman to be photographed. "They're beautiful," Martha said, her voice suddenly quavering. "But what's the occasion? It's not my birthday." She lifted the flowers to her face and inhaled their faint scent. Though the afternoon was cloudy, not sunny, and they were standing in her schoolyard, not picnicking in a field, the flowers transported Martha back to that wonderful day when Tom had kissed her. Had he been thinking about that when he'd chosen the flowers?

She looked at him, trying to read his expression, but all Martha saw was a raised eyebrow. It appeared that her question had surprised Tom, and he countered with one of his own. "Hasn't anyone ever given you a gift just because he wanted you to have it?"

Martha shook her head. "Not until today." Though her family had been a demonstrative one, lavishing affectionate touches on one another, presents had been exchanged on only two occasions: birthdays and Christmas. The fact that Tom had brought her something for no special reason brought tears to Martha's eyes. What a topsy-turvy day it had been! She had thought she had lost Tom forever, and here he was, surprising her with flowers. Martha touched the bluebonnets gently, bemused by Tom's gesture. "Whoever braided this is more talented than Carolyn and I used to be." Somehow, her voice sounded normal, though her heart was beating at twice its usual speed.

"I'll take that as a compliment."

Martha's gaze flew to Tom's face. "You made this?" The gift, which had touched her heart, was now infinitely more precious. Not only had Tom cared enough to bring her flowers, but he'd also invested his time in making those flowers special. "For me?"

Tom nodded, his expression once more sheepish. "You never told me what you and your sister did with the bluebonnets you braided, but I read somewhere that little girls like to wear flowers in their hair. I thought maybe big girls might like to, too."

The air was heavy with the threat of rain, and the breeze that had cooled the classroom had subsided. Even the mockingbird who normally serenaded the school was quiet. It was far from an ideal day, but Martha didn't care. All that mattered was the man who stood so close to her—her friend—and the wonderful gift he'd brought her.

She handed the flowers back to Tom and began to unpin her hat. "This big girl certainly wants to wear flowers." When she reached for the circlet, intending to place it on her head, Tom shook his head. He took a step forward, raising the flowers above her, then settled them on her hair as if she were a queen being crowned for the first time. It was the lightest of touches, a mere brushing of fingertips against her hair, and yet Martha could feel the warmth of Tom's fingers on her scalp, igniting fires that spread down her spine all the way to the tips of her toes. Did he have any idea what he was doing?

As an unwelcome thought assailed her, Martha shivered. Perhaps he did.

"The flowers are beautiful," she said when she had regained her composure. She touched the circlet, still not quite believing Tom had gone to the effort of picking and braiding flowers for her. It was a wonderfully romantic gesture, the type that troubadours in the Middle Ages celebrated in their songs. Though men occasionally gave flowers, a circlet of bluebonnets was the kind of gift that appeared in fairytales, not real life, and that made it all the more special. It made Martha feel as if she were special. But what if Tom had an ulterior motive? "I don't have enough words to tell you how pleased I am with the flowers. But," Martha said, her smile fading as she faced her fears, "I still won't let you use the photograph."

Tom blinked in apparent surprise. "That wasn't why I brought you flowers," he said, his voice low and filled with emotion. "I won't deny that I'd like you to be the Fourth of July Woman, but the flowers had nothing to do with that. They're for you, Martha. I wanted to show you that you're beautiful and special and that I was thinking of you."

"Oh." What else could she say?

* * *

The next afternoon, instead of meeting her at the foot of the school stairs as he normally did, Tom waited until the last pupil had left, then entered the schoolhouse. This time, though he kept one hand behind his back, as he had the day before, there was nothing sheepish about his expression. Today, Tom was smiling.

"Good afternoon," he said, extending a small box wrapped in white paper. "I hope you'll open it now."

Martha stared at him, not quite believing that he had brought her another gift. She had worn the circlet of bluebonnets home and, though she would normally have removed her hat once inside the house, had kept it on her head until she went to bed. Even then, she had placed it on her nightstand. If it wouldn't have precipitated a series of questions that she didn't want to answer, she would have worn it to school this morning. Flowers and now this. What had she done to deserve these gifts?

Martha unwrapped the package slowly so that she could savor each moment, then smiled at Tom when she opened the box and the delicious aroma of chocolate began to perfume the room. "How did you know that nougats were my favorite candy?" She knew that, though they had discussed hundreds of different topics, she and Tom had never ventured opinions about confectionery.

"Mr. Martin told me," Tom admitted. "I hoped his memory was accurate."

"It was." Each of the Wentworth children had favored a different type of candy, and nougats were hers. "It's been a long time since I had one." Martha set the box back on the desk, trying not to salivate at the wonderful smell. Her mother had always given her a box of nougats for her birthday, just as she had bought chocolate creams for Carolyn, covered cherries for Emily, and pralines for Theo. Since their parents' death, no one had continued the tradition, and though Martha had been inside Mr. Martin's store and passed the candy counter dozens of times, she had never bought any for herself. Candy—at least in Martha's opinion—was a treat, not something she gave herself.

"Go ahead. Eat one now."

Though the temptation was irresistible, Martha frowned as she looked at her fingers. "I need to wash my hands. I still have chalk dust on them."

Tom's smile turned into a lopsided grin. "Let me help." Before she could protest, he plucked a chocolate from the box and held it to her lips. "Go ahead," he repeated.

The chocolate was as delicious as Martha had remembered, a luscious coating over the nougat filling. It was a flavor combination she had discovered as a child and had never outgrown. Simply eating a piece of her special candy would have made the afternoon memorable, but the taste—undeniably delicious as it was—paled compared to the delight of having Tom feed that candy to her. For as he did, his fingertips brushed Martha's lips. It was a casual touch. He meant nothing by it, and yet that gentle touch was more wonderful than a whole box of chocolate. Her lips tingled, and suddenly the world shrank until there was no one in it but Tom and Martha, nothing more important than feeling the touch of his fingertips on her face. It was magic.

The next day, for the first time she could remember, Martha counted the minutes until she could dismiss the students. She loved teaching, and normally she enjoyed the time she spent with the pupils. Today all she could think about was Tom and how wonderful the time she had spent with him had been. More than once, Martha had caught herself staring at the big clock, and she suspected at least some of the students wondered why Mrs. York forgot that morning recess always began at ten o'clock. Though the logical part of her brain knew it was impossible, Martha would have sworn that the clock ticked more slowly than normal today. Soon it would be over. Soon the school day would end and she would be with Tom again.

Her pulse raced, just thinking of it. But when school ended, excitement was replaced by disappointment. Tom wasn't there waiting for the children to leave. Martha knew, because she had looked out the window, hoping to catch a glimpse of him standing under the oaks. That was where he stood each day. Not today. Something must have delayed him. Martha waited until the last of the pupils had gone before she looked again, and once again her stomach felt as if she'd eaten too many green apples. Tom still wasn't there. Fortunately, there were books to be shelved. Without Anna to help her, it took longer to ready the schoolhouse. Martha missed her friend's assistance and, even more, her companionship. Today, though, she did not grumble as she returned the books to the correct shelves, then straightened the schoolroom. Surely Tom would be there when she finished. He was not, and Martha had no further excuses for remaining in the schoolhouse.

Her heart heavy, she started for home. Something had happened to Tom. That was the only reason she could find for his absence. He wouldn't have left Canela without saying good-bye. Martha wouldn't believe that, not after the way he had treated her the past few days. Something was wrong. Something had happened to her friend Tom.

Martha was walking down Oak Street when she heard the sound of a car. She turned, and her heart sang with joy as she recognized Tom. The smile on his face said he was well. Her fears had been groundless.

"I'm sorry I'm late." Tom stopped the car and jumped out. Opening the passenger's door, he said, "Let me drive you home."

Though it was only a few blocks, Martha did not protest. There was no point in denying that she wanted to be with Tom, when the truth was, that was what she'd thought about all day. "I was afraid something had happened to you," she admitted as they drove slowly down Oak Street.

He looked astonished. "You were worried about me?"

Martha nodded. "I worry about all my friends."

Tom's lips thinned, as if somehow her words had displeased him. "I didn't mean to cause you any worry." He slowed the car even more, then reached into the back seat and pulled out a gaily wrapped package. "I hope you like this."

Another present! Martha stared in amazement.

"Go ahead, open it," Tom urged her.

The size and shape told Martha it was a book. Unwrapping it, she gasped in delight, for Tom had given her a book filled with paintings of Texas wildflowers. She had always loved books and spent so many hours reading that her sisters claimed she should have been a librarian, not a schoolteacher. But though she owned a number of books, none could compare to this one. "It's beautiful," Martha said, stroking the leather binding, then opening the book again to admire the paintings. "I've never had such a gorgeous book."

Tom pressed the clutch pedal as they rounded the corner. "I had to go to Victoria to get it," he said. "That's why I was late."

Martha looked at him, dumbfounded. Braiding bluebonnets, discovering her favorite candy, and now this. No one had ever done so much for her. "You're spoiling me," she protested.

"That's the idea."

"He's courting you."

Martha stared at Anna as if she were speaking a foreign language. The two women sat in front of Anna's small white house. With its window boxes and steeply pitched roof, Martha always thought of it as a Tyrolean chalet, a cottage that sat alone on its block. "Courting? That's nonsense." Though Martha had come to visit with her friend and to try to persuade her to return to school, today the conversation had turned to Tom and his gifts.

"It's not nonsense," Anna insisted. "Flowers, books, candy. Those are the traditional courting gifts."

Martha couldn't disagree. Though Henry had never courted her, Mrs. Wentworth had taught her daughters that those were the only gifts an unmarried woman could accept from her gentleman callers. The problem was that, even though those might be courting gifts, Tom wasn't courting Martha.

"He wants me to let him use my photograph," she told Anna. "This is part of his campaign to persuade me." Martha didn't want to believe that, but she could find no other explanation. Tom was *not* courting her. He was not a marrying man, and even if he were, she was not the wife he would choose.

The older woman's eyes sparkled with something that, under other circumstances, Martha might have identified as amusement. "You're mistaken, my friend. I've seen the way that man looks at you. He's in love with you, Martha, just as you're in love with him."

Anna was wrong. Absolutely, positively wrong. Love was one thing. Martha admitted that she loved Tom—as a friend. Being in love was something very different.

"It's you who are mistaken," Martha said as mildly as she could. There was no point in arguing with Anna. When the woman made up her mind, nothing would change it.

"I'm not blind," Anna insisted. "I know what I've seen."

Martha couldn't let her continue to believe such nonsense. "I care about Tom," she admitted, "but it's not the way I felt about Henry."

Anna nodded, her expression seeming to say that Martha had not surprised her. "I know," she said.

The woman could be infuriating. She was also mistaken. "I loved Henry."

Anna smiled again. "I know."

* * *

It had been more difficult than he'd expected. Tom took the laundry that Mrs. Bradley had washed for him and began to toss it into a bureau drawer. He needed to do something—anything—to stop thinking about tonight. This whole courting business was more complicated than he'd ever dreamt. It might come naturally to some men, but Tom was not one of those fortunate men. At first he had had no idea what to do. He couldn't simply declare his intentions to Martha. He couldn't walk up to her and say, "I want to marry you." Tom might not know a lot about courting rituals, but he knew that approach was doomed. And so, though he knew he would have to listen to her crowing with delight, he had telephoned his mother.

Of course, he had had to leave Canela to do that. Tom wasn't going to have someone on the Canela party line just happen to overhear that particular conversation. No, sirree. His plans wouldn't have much chance of success if the Canela grapevine announced his intentions before he had a chance to implement them. Once she'd recovered from her initial shock, his mother had been happy to offer advice. He had taken it, too. Flowers, books, and candy, Mother had said. As far as Tom could tell, Martha liked the gifts. She had certainly acted as if she did. She had worn that silly coronet of flowers, her smile as bright as if he'd given her a jeweled crown, and she'd oohed and aahed over the book.

Tom had to admit that his favorite gift had been the candy. He wasn't a big fan of chocolate nougats, but there was no denying that he had enjoyed the one that Martha had fed him. Who would have thought that something could taste so good, just because a pretty woman fed it to him? She had been careful, though, and her fingers hadn't touched his lips the way his had touched hers. More's the pity. It had taken all the willpower Tom possessed to pull his hand away from Martha's lips. They'd felt so soft against his fingertips, and that had reminded him of how soft those lips had felt against his. He wanted to kiss her again. Oh, how he wanted to kiss her! He'd do that soon, but not too soon. He couldn't rush this courting business. Mother had warned him about that.

Tom closed the drawer and stared at the package that had arrived today. Mother had been surprised when he had asked for it, and for a moment Tom had thought she was going to insist that he come to Rochester to get it. But she hadn't. The package was here, Sidney had agreed that the photographs of Canela were good enough for a rotogravure, and Tom was as ready as he would ever be. Tonight was the night. If only he could muster the courage to say the words that would change his life forever.

Tom reached for his stack of prints. Perhaps if he looked at The Photograph he'd be able to dissolve the lump that had lodged in the pit of his stomach. And perhaps he'd find a way to convince Martha to be his Fourth of July Woman. Perhaps he should have told her the truth, that his whole career depended on that picture, but he couldn't. After all, a man had his pride. A man wanted the woman he loved to respect him, to believe he was successful. A man shouldn't have to beg.

Tom leafed through the pictures. That was odd. He was certain it was in the first half. He continued looking. When he reached the bottom, his heart began to pound. It had to be there. Perhaps it was stuck to another print.

He went through the stack again, more slowly this time. And when he reached the bottom, the pounding of his heart had turned into an ominous thudding. It wasn't here. He hadn't lost it. Tom was certain of that. The only explanation—the one he didn't want to consider—was that he had somehow sent it to Sidney by mistake. That would explain why Sidney hadn't asked about the Fourth of July Woman when he'd discussed the Canela rotogravure pictures. Sidney had been more terse than usual, leading Tom to surmise that his editor was in a hurry. He had thought that was the reason Sidney hadn't demanded Martha's picture. Now Tom feared there was another reason.

He pulled out his watch. If he hurried, he could get to the telegraph station before it closed. He would send Sidney a message, telling him not to under any circumstances use pictures of the blond. Sidney wouldn't like the message, but the man was honorable. He wouldn't print a photograph without Tom's approval. And maybe, if tonight went the way Tom hoped, Martha would say yes to two very different questions.

Martha slid her feet into her pumps, then turned slowly in front of the cheval mirror, considering her reflection. How she wished she were the same size as Carolyn. If she were, she could have borrowed one of her sister's pretty frocks. But wishing didn't make Martha three inches taller, and so she was going to have to wear a dress Tom had already seen. Martha had tried to buy a new dress, but Ida Bloom had nothing in her size. The shopkeeper had shown her the few dresses that remained, reminding her that even though she couldn't sell Martha a frock suitable for tonight's dinner, she was still planning to sew her wedding dress.

Martha didn't need a wedding gown. What she needed was a new dress to wear to the country club tonight. Though Tom hadn't said it, she suspected that this was a farewell dinner. It might be foolish, but she wanted his last memory of her to be one of her in a pretty new dress. This one was pretty. The problem was, he'd seen it the last time they'd gone to the country club.

"You're perfect!" Tom said as she joined him on the front porch. He was standing with one hand behind his back. Surely he had not brought her another gift! Tom's gaze moved from the top of Martha's head to her freshly polished shoes. "Perfect," he repeated.

Though she could feel the color rush to her cheeks, Martha smiled, remembering the first time she had heard Tom say that. "It wasn't true the day we met, and it isn't true now."

"I told you you were wrong then, and you're wrong to-night, but I'm not going to argue." Tom brought his hand forward and gave her a corsage. "I had hoped you'd wear that dress again tonight," he said. Though the flowers were white daisies, the ribbon was the exact shade of Martha's gown, making it evident that he'd once more invested time in planning the perfect gift for her. Suddenly, Martha didn't mind that she had been unable to find a new dress or that Carolyn's pretty frocks hadn't fit her.

"Thank you, Tom. The flowers are beautiful."

"No more beautiful than you."

Martha busied herself pinning the flowers to her dress. "You're making me blush."

Tom's chuckle warmed her as much as his compliment. "It's deliberate," he admitted as he opened the door to the Model T and ushered her into the passenger's seat. "You're even more beautiful when you blush."

Afterwards, Martha couldn't remember what they had eaten or what they had said. Instead, she remembered how Tom's eyes sparkled when he laughed and how when he had pursed his lips in apparent contemplation all she could think about was how wonderful those lips had felt pressed against hers. She remembered how he held his knife and the excitement those fingers had generated when they'd touched her hair. She remembered that his voice was warm and that he had made her feel as if she were indeed beautiful. But mostly Martha remembered what happened after dinner.

When they had finished their meal, Tom suggested they walk outside. It was a soft spring night, the ideal time for a stroll, and the country club was the perfect place. Its grounds were beautifully groomed, with paths leading to a small pond, a formal garden and a fanciful gazebo. It was the gazebo that Tom chose as their destination. They walked slowly, enjoying the warm air and the scents of flowers. Martha placed her hand on Tom's arm as she often did when they walked. Tonight was different, though. Tonight, Martha felt as if tension were radiating from Tom's arm. Could it be that he was dreading their parting as much as she? Though he had not mentioned leaving, Martha could not dismiss the belief that tonight would be Tom's last night in Canela.

"I heard from Sidney today," he said when they were seated on one of the wrought iron benches inside the gazebo.

Martha had always liked the gazebo. The delicate white structure seemed like something out of a fairytale, and that appealed to her. So, too, did its location on top of a small hill. From here, she could see the whole town of Canela. It was far enough away that the houses looked like toys but close enough that she could identify them. There was her own house, Mrs. Bleeker's, and on the other side of town, the school and Anna's cottage. Martha would think about the beauty of her hometown, not the fact that Tom would soon be leaving.

"Did Sidney like the photographs?" Though she had doubted it possible, her voice sounded perfectly normal. By some miracle, none of her distress was reflected in it.

"He seemed to. He told me to send the rest of the pictures, and Sidney wouldn't have done that if he wasn't interested."

"Then you'll be leaving." Though Martha hated pronouncing the words, there was no point in pretending this wasn't their farewell. She had known that it was inevitable. What she hadn't known was how empty she would feel inside at the thought of Tom's leaving.

"There's no reason to stay." Surely he should have a little regret. Instead, Tom acted as if he were discussing Mr. Martin's latest fishing expedition.

An owl hooted, its plaintive cry sounding as sorrowful as she felt. Martha bit her lip. She wouldn't cry. She wouldn't. "I'll miss you." The words spilled out before she could stop them.

Tom took her right hand in his, raising her to her feet. "You don't have to."

"It's not as if I have a choice." Did he think she wanted to feel this way? Did he think she enjoyed the fact that everyone she loved went away?

"You do have a choice." Tom gazed at her for a long moment, and in the bright moonlight she saw an unfamiliar expression reflected in his eyes. It startled her with its intensity, igniting a flame deep inside her. Tom nodded slowly, then, still holding her hand, he dropped to his knees. "I don't want to leave without you." He looked up at her, his expression solemn. "I never thought I'd say this, but I've changed in ways I would not have believed possible since I came to Canela. I never thought I was lonely, but now I realize that I no longer want to travel alone." He tightened the grip on her hand. "Martha, I want you by my side today, tomorrow, and always. Will you marry me?"

Tears sprang to Martha's eyes as she stared at the man she loved, the man who had just said the words she longed to hear. Until he had pronounced them, she hadn't realized that that was what she wanted—to marry Tom and live happily ever after with him. If only that were possible!

"I wish I could marry you, but I can't."

Tom rose and looked down at her. "Why not?" he asked softly. He reached for her other hand and held it as he waited for her answer.

Martha took a deep breath, trying to calm herself. The image of herself and Tom together was so compelling that it hurt to refuse him. It would be a dream come true, being Tom's wife, sharing his life. If only it were possible! But dreams, Martha knew, rarely came true. "You'd expect me to leave Canela." He had been honest about that. "I can't do it, Tom. The town needs me, and I need it. This is my home. This is where I belong."

He gripped her hands. "What about me? I need you."

"You don't need me. You don't need anyone." He wanted her with him. She understood that. But wanting wasn't the same as needing, and wanting wasn't the same as loving. Tom wanted her, but that wasn't enough.

"You're wrong, Martha, I—" Tom glanced behind her, a horrified look on his face. "What's that?"

Martha spun around and looked down at the town, and as she did, she gasped. "It's Anna's house. It's on fire!"

Chapter Ten

M
artha hadn't realized that a Model T could go so fast.
She wasn't sure what Tom was doing to it, but it felt as if
they were flying along the roads. They had come down the
hill so quickly that Martha had breathed a silent prayer that
Tom would be able to stop at the bottom. Though he
stopped, her fears did not subside when they reached level
ground, for he took one turn so quickly that Martha was
afraid the car would topple onto its side. Her heart pounding wildly, she barely breathed until, sooner than she had
thought possible, they were in front of Anna's house.

Martha wasn't prepared for the sight. She had seen the
flames from the gazebo and had smelled the smoke as they
raced back into town. She had thought she knew what to
expect, but she was mistaken. Never had she seen devas-
tation like this. If she hadn't known better, Martha might
have believed that she was looking at the ruins of a French
village after enemy shelling.

The flames that she and Tom had seen were doused, but
the damage was already done. What had been a small frame
house was now a charred ruin. Soot, ashes and cinders were
everywhere. So, too, it seemed was half the town. Though

the effort appeared futile to Martha, people were still tossing buckets of water on the now smoldering house.

"Oh, Tom!" Martha shuddered at the horror of the scene. As soon as he stopped the car, she leaped out and ran into the crowd, searching for her friend. Where was Anna? Though the townspeople were working to control the fire, no one seemed to know Anna's whereabouts. Fear lodged deep in Martha's heart as she realized that Anna might be trapped inside. *No!* she cried silently. It couldn't be.

"Anna!" This time Martha shouted aloud. Several people shook their heads, indicating that they had not seen her. Then Hugh Ashton, who was leading the fire brigade, said, "There was no one inside."

Thank heavens! Perhaps Anna had gone for one of the nighttime walks that she enjoyed. Martha searched the perimeter, and as she did, she saw a woman emerge from the stand of trees at the end of the street. Anna! She was safe! Martha raced to her friend and enfolded her in her arms.

"Mein haus!" Anna cried. *"Alles ist weg."*

The anguish she heard in Anna's voice wrenched Martha's heart. It was true that the house and all that was in it were gone. "You're safe," she said. "That's all that matters. The house can be replaced." If there was one thing the war had taught Martha, it was that, though possessions might seem valuable, the only thing of any real importance was human life. That was infinitely precious.

But Anna would not be consoled. "Everything we had, Kurt and I, it's all gone. Where will I live? What will I do?"

As one of the walls began to crumble, Martha pulled Anna further from the rubble. Dimly, she was aware of Tom carrying his camera and tripod and of the occasional flash as he took a photograph. The bucket brigade continued, with people drawing water from Anna's well.

"There's plenty of room in my house," Martha told Anna. "You can live with me."

The older woman shook her head and took a step away. "It wouldn't be safe. It might happen again." Though she had not reverted to German, Anna's accent was heavier than normal.

"What do you mean?" Anna sounded as if she thought there might be a second fire and that the next time it would be Martha's house that went up in flames. "Accidents happen, but not very often." This was the first major fire that Martha could remember. There had been a lightning strike once that had burned a barn, but nothing of this magnitude.

"This was no accident. Someone set the fire." Anna was adamant. "Someone wanted to hurt me. I think they wanted to kill me."

Martha looked at the townspeople, the men and women who were even now pouring water on the ruins of Anna's house. They were good people, good neighbors. "You must be mistaken, Anna. No one in Canela is that evil."

It was midmorning when Martha heard the knock on the door. Though Anna had protested, Martha had insisted that her friend come home with her, telling her she had to sleep somewhere. Tom had chimed in, declaring that Anna would be doing Martha a favor. "She won't sleep if she's worrying about you."

"Ja." Anna had nodded solemnly. "That is true." With no further protests, she had climbed into Tom's car and allowed him to drive her and Martha to the house on Chestnut Street. Anna had been so silent on the ride that Martha had wondered whether she had fallen asleep. But before either of them slept, they spent an hour sitting at the kitchen table, drinking warm milk and talking about ordinary things. Anna did not refer to the fire, and Martha did not tell her friend that she had received her first marriage proposal.

Though Martha suspected Anna would not be surprised by the fact that Tom had asked Martha to marry him, she imagined the older woman would not believe this was the first time a man had proposed to Martha. It was. Though she had married Henry York, he had never actually asked for Martha's hand. They'd loved each other for so long that they—like everyone else in Canela—had assumed that marriage was inevitable. The closest Henry had come to a proposal was the day he'd asked Martha when she thought they ought to get married. When, not whether. It hadn't been romantic, but Martha hadn't needed romance. She was marrying her sweetheart; fancy words weren't important. This time was different. She had received fancy words last night, and all they had brought was heartache. Tom was asking too much; she simply could not give all that he'd asked.

Martha opened the door, nodding when she saw that the visitor was Tom. She had expected him to return. As she knew from his frequent requests to use her photograph as the Fourth of July Woman, Tom was not a man who gave up easily.

"We didn't finish our conversation last night," he said after he'd asked about Anna and had received Martha's assurance that there was nothing more he could do for her. Though Anna's presence in the house meant that they were theoretically chaperoned, Martha did not invite Tom inside. Instead, she motioned to the front porch swing. A faint scent of smoke still hung in the air, an unwelcome reminder of last night's tragedy, and Martha wondered if she'd ever be able to smell smoke without remembering the look of horror on Anna's face when she had seen her house.

"I hope you've reconsidered," Tom said when they were seated. He took Martha's hands in his and smiled at her.

Though she tried to return the smile, the lump in Martha's throat made it difficult. She had slept only an hour or two, too distracted by thoughts of the fire and Tom's proposal to relax for more than a few minutes at a time. She loved Tom, and with the clarity that came after hours of pacing the floor, Martha knew that she loved him not as a friend but as the man she wanted to marry. When Henry had died, Martha had accepted the fact that she would never remarry, that she would never find another man to love. She'd been half right. She had found the man, but she couldn't marry him.

"I want to marry you, Martha." Tom kept his gaze fixed on her, and she saw nothing but sincerity in his eyes. "I want us to spend the rest of our lives together."

Martha wanted that, too. But, though it hurt almost unbearably to admit it, she knew that wasn't possible. Two very large obstacles stood between them and the happily ever after that Martha wanted with all her heart. The first was that they differed in their definitions of how they would spend the life that they shared. "You won't stay here."

In the distance a songbird trilled. It sounded happy, as if it were celebrating the beautiful morning. Tom's smile faded, and the expression she saw on his face told Martha more clearly than words that he was not happy with her response.

"How could I support us if I didn't travel? Photography is what I do. It's my life."

"And Canela is my life." Martha looked at the neighboring houses. Other than the few months she'd been married to Henry, she had seen those houses every day of her life. She couldn't imagine waking up in a different town each day, not having a place to call home, being surrounded by strangers, having nothing to do other than be the wife of a man who wanted her, who claimed he needed her, but who did not love her. Martha had friends in Canela, and when the war was over, she would once again have family. This was her life, the only one she'd ever known. She couldn't give that up for a man who didn't love her.

That was the second obstacle—the truly insurmountable

one—that blocked the path to happiness. Though Martha loved Tom, that love was not returned.

Tom's eyes were serious as he studied her face. "I'm asking you to share my life, to become part of it. Martha, I want us to have a future together."

This was what she had expected as she had paced the floor. There would be no happy ending. Slowly, Martha shook her head. "I want to marry you, Tom. I do. But I cannot leave Canela. The peripatetic life is perfect for you, but it would be wrong for me. I need a home."

Tom tightened his grip on her hands. "I can't believe you're willing to throw away our chance at happiness."

"I don't think it would last." That was the problem. In Martha's experience, happiness was fleeting. Her marriage had ended all too soon; her parents had died far too young; even her ties to her siblings had been broken by this horrible war. There was no reason to believe that marriage to Tom would be the start of happily ever after.

"I'd make you happy, Martha." Tom's eyes were serious as he gazed at her. "I'd do everything in my power to make you happy."

She nodded. "I know you would. The problem is me, not you. I can't imagine living anywhere but here. I can't imagine not having a home."

"We'd be together."

"That would be wonderful, but what if the happiness fades? I'm afraid that I'd start to blame you, and then neither of us would be happy."

The songbird continued to serenade his unseen partner. On another day, Martha would have smiled at the warbling. Today she felt as if nothing could make her smile.

"Life doesn't come with guarantees." Tom spoke slowly, as if that would persuade her. "I can't promise you'll be happy. All I can promise is that I'll do my very best to make you happy. The rest is up to you, Martha. You have to be willing to take a risk."

Martha closed her eyes for a second, trying to imagine the life Tom was offering. It wouldn't work. She knew that, as surely as she knew that the sun would rise each morning. She opened her eyes and fixed her gaze on Tom. How wonderful it would be to see his face each morning and every night! But that was an impossible dream.

"If you loved me," Martha said softly, "you wouldn't ask me to leave."

The flash of anger that crossed Tom's face surprised her. "What does love have to do with it?" he demanded. "I'm being practical, Martha. The way I earn my living is by taking pictures, and I've taken all I can here."

He didn't understand, and it seemed he never would. "Give me some more time," she pleaded. "Let me get Anna settled." Martha didn't want to believe that Anna was in any further danger, but the captain of the firemen had confirmed that the fire was deliberately set. Until Martha knew that her friend was safe, that whoever had destroyed her house was caught and punished, she could not consider leaving. By then maybe she would have found a way to create the happy ending she wanted for herself and Tom.

Tom shook his head. "If it wasn't Anna, it would be someone else, another excuse not to leave this town."

Martha bridled. "That's not true." They weren't excuses.

"Isn't it?" Though Tom kept his voice low, there was a fierceness in it that told her he was as angry as she. "You don't have a life of your own. Everything you do revolves around this town that you think is so perfect. The truth is, it isn't perfect, and I have the proof."

He reached for the envelope he had placed on the porch floor and pulled out a sheaf of photographs. Intermingled with the pictures of Anna's burning house were shots of the townspeople. Though many were working intently, trying to extinguish the fire, several wore expressions that could only be described as satisfied.

Martha stared at them in horror. Tom's photographs confirmed what Hugh Ashton had said, that the fire was no accident. "What are you going to do with these?" she asked. Though the proof was in front of her, Martha found it difficult to believe that anyone in Canela would take pleasure from the destruction of Anna's home.

Tom shrugged as if the answer should be apparent. "I'm going to mail them to Sidney and have him include several of them in the rotogravure."

Though she hadn't thought it possible, Martha's horror increased. It was bad enough to know that there was evil in Canela, but to put that on display for the rest of the country was unthinkable.

"You can't do that."

"I can, and I will." Tom took the pictures from Martha's hand. "What's the matter?" he asked, his voice once more harsh with anger. "Are you afraid that others will see the true Canela and realize that it's not perfect?"

He was misinterpreting her words. Of course, she knew her hometown wasn't perfect. Nothing was. But if these pictures were included in the story, people would believe that arson and hatred were a part of daily life in Canela. That simply wasn't true.

Before she could speak, Tom continued. "Maybe if you took off those rose-colored glasses you seem to be wearing, you'd see that Canela is like every other town in this country. It has good and bad, and they're mixed together." Martha started to reply, but Tom held up his hand, mimicking the gesture she used when she wanted the children's attention. "If you take those glasses off long enough, you might even realize that your marriage to Saint Henry wasn't perfect."

He had gone too far. Horror, anger, and sorrow had formed a dangerous mixture, and Tom's final words had struck the spark that ignited combustion. "Don't you dare talk about my marriage." Martha's voice was low but seething with anger. "You don't know anything about it. How could you? You wouldn't recognize love if it came up to you and grabbed your hand." She shook her head, forbidding him to speak. "I feel sorry for you, Tom. I really do, but I can't marry a man who thinks of no one but himself." And she couldn't stay here a minute longer. Martha rose. "You wanted my answer. Here it is. I won't marry you, Tom. Not today, not next month, not ever."

Without a backward glance, she walked into her house, not caring that the door slammed behind her. Fury propelled her up the stairs and into her bedroom. She yanked open the bureau drawer and grabbed the photograph Tom had taken of her on her front porch, the one he claimed was the best one he'd ever taken. Slowly and deliberately, Martha ripped it into tiny shreds. Then, and only then, did she let herself weep.

She was the most infuriating woman he'd ever met. Tom gripped the steering wheel. Though the road was moderately smooth, he almost wished for rocks and potholes. Jolting through them might improve his disposition. It was certain that thinking of Martha would do nothing to sweeten his mood.

He didn't understand her; that was for sure. Martha was smart about so many things, but she was blind as could be where her own happiness was concerned. She spent her days worrying about others' lives, but she couldn't see that she was wasting her own, throwing away her chance at happiness. A smart woman didn't do that.

A smart woman didn't let herself get so confused that she blamed someone else, either. Tom couldn't figure out why she thought everything was his fault. For Pete's sake, he'd done everything he could. What more did she expect from him? He'd already bared his soul to her. Did she think it was easy, admitting how much she'd changed his life? He'd already asked her to marry him. He'd even followed his mother's instructions and had done that on bended knee, although it was the silliest position he could imagine. He'd done all that, and what had Martha done? She'd thrown it all back in his face.

Imagine! She'd claimed he didn't love her. What on earth made her think that? Why else would he have asked her to marry him? Why else would he be carrying his grandmother's ring in his pocket, waiting to slip it on Martha's finger? Why else?

He'd done all that, and it still wasn't enough. She wanted him to give up his career, everything he'd worked for, and spend the rest of his life in Canela. Tom jerked the steering wheel and felt a moment of satisfaction as the car lurched to the right. He wouldn't do it. Canela might be the Friendliest Little Town in East Texas, but it wasn't his town, and it never would be. No, sirree. That was one mistake he wasn't going to make.

He was gone. Martha put a drop of water on the griddle, nodding slightly when it danced. It was hot enough for pancakes. She poured the batter carefully, making four cakes. Though she had made a mess of her life, perhaps she could succeed at a simple task like cooking breakfast. She had heard Anna stirring, and even though it was almost noon, she wanted to give her friend a normal breakfast. Maybe then Anna's day would be better than Martha's.

She wouldn't ever see him again. The thought reverberated through Martha's mind, seemingly louder with each repetition. Tom was gone, and it was her fault. Worse than the fact that he was gone was the way they had parted. In anger. Martha's mother had taught her and her siblings that it was wrong to let the sun set on their anger. It appeared that was one lesson Martha hadn't learned, for the sun would set on her hasty words not just once but for the rest of her life.

How she wished she could see Tom again! Just once. Just long enough to make amends. She couldn't marry him, of course. She couldn't change her life for him. The answer she gave him wouldn't change, but the way she delivered it would.

Martha watched bubbles forming in the pancakes and knew it was time to turn them. If only she could turn back the clock. If only she hadn't been so angry. If only she hadn't said those cruel words. Tom was wrong about Canela. He had never lived in a small town, and so he didn't understand the ties that bound the residents together. He was mistaken, badly mistaken, but that was no excuse for lashing out at him the way she had. Tom wasn't a bad man, yet Martha had acted as if he were. She had accused him of being selfish and unable to love, when the truth was, he was simply acting the way many only children did.

Martha was a schoolteacher. As such, she knew she couldn't expect her pupils to master a subject unless she had taught it. Learning to share and to understand others were lessons Tom still needed. That didn't make him bad, and it most definitely didn't mean that he deserved to be berated. Martha couldn't undo the words she'd spoken, but if she could, she'd apologize for them.

"You're miserable without that man," Anna said a few minutes later as she poured syrup on her pancakes. Though her face was still unusually pale, Anna appeared calm. Her voice had been level when she'd spoken of her house. It was only now when she studied Martha's expression that she displayed emotion.

Martha couldn't deny her friend's allegations. "I'm unhappy because of the things I said to Tom," she agreed. Impulsively, she had told Anna of Tom's proposal and her own refusal and had had to listen to Anna tell her she was foolish. "We have no future together," Martha said, refuting Anna's arguments. "I know that. But I wish I'd thanked Tom for the things he's done for all of us: arranging for the carousel, helping me with the play, talking to the children. . . ." Martha's voice trailed off as she thought of the many ways Tom had brightened life in Canela. In just a short time, he'd made a considerable impression on the town. He had changed things in a positive way.

"He's a good man." Anna stirred her coffee, tasted it, then added another drop of milk.

"I know. Tom's not the right man for me, but he's still a good man." Martha cut a piece of pancake. "I'd like to send him a letter of apology." That would make her feel better, and perhaps it would help Tom, too. "The problem is, I don't have his address."

"Send the letter to the gazette."

Martha considered that possibility but dismissed it. "I couldn't do that. What if someone opened the letter?" She didn't want anyone else to read her apology. "Still . . ." Martha chewed slowly, weighing Anna's suggestion. "Tom's editor will have his address," she said at last. "I'll call him."

An hour later, Martha was finally connected to the *Gainey Gazette*'s office.

"This is Sidney Vesper." The man sounded harried.

"You don't know me, Mr. Vesper, but my name is Martha York, and I live in Canela, Texas."

There was a moment of silence. "Canela . . . ah, yes, the town Tom Fleming wants to make famous." Before Martha could say anything more, Sidney continued, "I don't know why you're calling, Miss York, but you could do me a favor. The next time you see Tom Fleming, tell him he'd better get me the picture he promised or he'll never sell another photograph to the *Gazette*."

As the editor's words registered, Martha felt the blood drain from her face. "Are you referring to the Fourth of July Woman?"

"Exactly." Though there was a crackling on the phone line, Martha had little difficulty hearing Sidney. "I'll admit that I was opposed to the idea at first, but Tom convinced me. Then I made the mistake of mentioning it to my publisher." Martha gripped the telephone receiver. Though she did not like what she was hearing, she didn't want to miss a single word. Sidney continued, "My boss agreed with Tom that it's what the *Gainey Gazette* needs. He wants to see that picture, and so do I." The editor took a breath. "You tell Tom I wasn't joking. If I don't have the Fourth of July Woman's picture on my desk in ten days, his career with me is over." The man paused again. "Now, Miss York, what was it you wanted?"

"Nothing. Nothing at all."

For a long moment, Martha stared at the telephone, replaying the editor's words, trying to dissolve the horrible lump that had lodged in her throat. If only she'd known! She stumbled back to the kitchen where Anna was sipping her second cup of coffee.

"Oh, Anna." Martha sank into one of the chairs and covered her face with her hands. "I was so wrong about Tom. I accused him of being selfish, but he wasn't." If he had been selfish, he would have used the photograph, even without her permission. She had been the one who'd been selfish, withholding the one thing that could help the man she loved. "I wouldn't believe him when he said he needed the picture of me to save his career." Martha had thought it a ploy, never dreaming that Tom had told her the truth.

Anna's blue eyes were sober as she regarded Martha. "I didn't think you would even consider letting him use the picture."

"That's what I said, but if I'd known how important it was to Tom, I'd have agreed."

Anna nodded slowly. "You can still do that."

"How?"

"You told me Tom gave you the photograph. Send it to his editor. The man won't care whether it comes from Tom or you."

"I can't." Martha grimaced as she pronounced the words. "I destroyed it."

Chapter Eleven

She had barely cleared the breakfast dishes when she heard a firm knock on the front door. Martha spun around so quickly that her arm caught the handle of the coffeepot, and it tumbled into the sink, clattering as it landed against the cutlery. Tom? Could it be Tom? Her heart racing with anticipation, she hurried toward the door. It wasn't Tom. Of course it wasn't Tom. He would never come back. But, though she tried to steel herself for disappointment, Martha couldn't help smiling as she opened the door. This could be her chance to undo at least one of her mistakes.

Her smile faded as she saw that her visitor was not Tom but Ida Bloom. The proprietor of the Canela Dress Emporium held a large sack in one hand and had a clothing bag draped over the other arm.

"Is Anna still here?" Though Miss Bloom smiled, the smile did not reach her eyes, and her expression looked as strained as Martha felt. "Is she all right?"

Nodding in response to both questions, Martha gestured toward the kitchen. "Anna, you have a visitor." She guided Miss Bloom toward the back of the house.

Ida Bloom plopped the sack on the floor, then laid the dress bag over the back of a chair. "I heard what hap-

157

pened," she said solemnly as she pulled a dress from the garment bag. "It's not the color I would have chosen for you," she said, gesturing toward the light green frock that had once graced the front window of the Dress Emporium, "but I believe it will fit. If not, I can alter it for you."

Anna fingered the fine muslin. "I'm not certain when I'll be able to pay you," she said as she held the green dress in front of her. It was, Martha noted, the right length for her friend, and it appeared to be the right size, too. Years of experience had made Ida Bloom a good judge of women's sizes.

"Please do not insult me." Ida Bloom handed Anna a navy silk gown. The dark color flattered Anna's blond hair and blue eyes, and a faint blush stained her cheeks as she touched the navy silk almost reverently. Anna had never, Martha knew, owned a silk dress. She shook her head slowly. "It is too expensive."

Miss Bloom pursed her lips. "Nonsense. These are gifts," she said. When Anna appeared speechless, the dressmaker continued softly, "You would have done the same for me." She gestured toward the sack. "There are some unmentionables in here. I knew you would need them, too."

Tears filled Anna's eyes. "I don't know what to say, other than thank you."

Ida Bloom shook her head. "No thanks are necessary."

When Anna took her new clothing upstairs, Martha resumed dishwashing. Ten minutes later she heard another knock. It was Mrs. Bleeker, her next-door neighbor, carrying another bag. "You'll be doing me a favor if you take these shoes," she said as she showed Anna a pair of high-button boots. "They pinch my toes something fierce." While Martha doubted the story, since her neighbor had bought the shoes only a few weeks earlier and had worn them to church with no apparent discomfort, she appreciated the way Mrs. Bleeker was trying to salvage Anna's pride. Like Miss Bloom, she seemed to understand that while Anna had lost all her possessions, she did not want to accept charity. Anna had always been fiercely independent, a woman who gave rather than took.

Miss Bloom and Mrs. Bleeker were the vanguard. By the end of the day, Martha's parlor was filled with items that Canela's citizens had brought for Anna. In addition to clothing, the offerings included dishes, pans, and even a rocking chair.

When Mrs. Lewis, the mayor's wife, arrived shortly before dinner, she was the first to come empty-handed. It was a relief, for Martha was not certain where she would put another roaster, and her kitchen was filled with an almost overwhelming selection of freshly baked cakes and pies along with enough canned goods to feed Martha and Anna for a month.

Mrs. Lewis accepted a glass of the lemonade Martha had offered to all the visitors, then turned to Anna. "I know Martha is happy to share her house with you, and the Good Lord knows she has enough empty rooms here." The mayor's wife gestured toward the second floor. "Sometimes, though, it's difficult for two grown women to share a house." Giving Anna a conspiratorial smile, she continued, "You could rebuild your house, but that will take a while." What Mrs. Lewis didn't say was that it also required money, and that was something Anna did not have.

The mayor's wife sipped her lemonade, complimenting Martha on the flavor as if this were an ordinary social visit. Then she turned back to Anna. "I don't want you to feel that you must accept, but there's a cottage at the back of our yard. When she was still alive, my mother used to live there. It's not as large as yours was, but it would give you privacy if you didn't want to impose on Martha." Had the mayor's wife overhead Anna's protests last night, or did she simply realize how much Anna hated being what she considered a burden? The question was how much rent the Lewises would charge.

Anna nodded slowly, obviously considering the suggestion. As she opened her mouth to reply, Mrs. Lewis spoke. "Please hear me out. The cottage has been empty for six years now. I haven't wanted to go in it since Mama died, so I fear it's dirty and needs some repairs. Mr. Lewis and I talked about it this morning. If you'd be willing to take care of it, we'd like to put the deed in your name."

The offer was incredibly generous but—like Mrs. Bleeker's gift of her new shoes—phrased in a way that did not insult Anna. Martha hoped she would accept.

Anna stared at Mrs. Lewis for a long moment, as if trying to understand the motives behind her words. "You would do that for me?"

The mayor's wife nodded. "It's very simple, Anna. We don't want you to leave Canela."

Anna, a woman not known for her physical gestures, reached for Mrs. Lewis's hand and held it between both of hers. *"Danke schön,"* she said. Then she shook her head, correcting herself for her lapse into her native language. "Thank you," she repeated in English.

Martha smiled and, for the hundredth time that day, wished Tom were here. If he were here, she could apologize for her harsh words, she could tell him to send Mr. Vesper the Fourth of July Woman picture, and—just as importantly—she could show him that Canela was filled with kindhearted people. Though her home wasn't perfect, surely today's outpouring of generosity proved its inherent goodness. But Tom did not come, and for several hours, neither did anyone else.

The sun was setting when Mr. Martin entered the house, an envelope in his hand. "I would have been here sooner," he explained, "but I couldn't close the store, not when half the ladies in Canela were making extra trips." The shopkeeper's eyes twinkled as if he knew that much of the merchandise he'd sold today had found its way to Martha's parlor. "I remembered that my wife put a box of old photographs in the attic," he told Anna. "It took me a while to find it, but I thought you might like this one."

He pulled the photo from the envelope and handed it to Anna. It was, Martha saw, an ordinary picture, somewhat faded by time. Compared to Tom's work, this one appeared distinctly amateur. The lighting was wrong, and one of the subjects was out of focus. Anna, Martha knew instinctively, saw none of the flaws. To her the photograph would be priceless, for it captured the image of six men standing in front of Mr. Martin's store. One of those men was Anna's husband.

"Kurt! My Kurt!" For the first time that day, the tears that had been so close to the surface began to fall, and Anna sobbed as she stared at the only tangible reminder she had of her beloved spouse.

"I thought she'd like it." Mr. Martin shuffled his feet, his discomfort obvious.

"She does," Martha assured him as Anna's tears continued to flow. They had been building all day, but it had taken the shopkeeper's kindness to release them.

He shook his head. "I never will understand women."

Though the stream of visitors turned into a trickle, by the end of the week, almost everyone in Canela had found a reason to visit Martha's house. Some merely expressed their sorrow over Anna's loss. Others brought food or household goods. Only one family was conspicuous by their absence: the Bradleys. Martha wasn't surprised, for Hank Bradley had been one of the people whose satisfied smile Tom had caught in his photographs of the fire. Hank might not have been the one who ignited it, but Martha had no doubt he believed Anna deserved to lose her home and that she should return to Germany. It was, therefore, a surprise when Martha left the schoolhouse on Friday and saw Mrs. Bradley approaching her.

"Do you know how to reach Tom?" Mrs. Bradley asked without preamble.

Martha shook her head. Though she wondered why his former landlady wanted to contact him, she wouldn't ask.

"I found this." Mrs. Bradley reached into her reticule and pulled out a photograph. "I was cleaning his room yesterday and saw it under the bureau. I couldn't figure out how it got there, 'cause Tom was mighty particular about his photographs." Color rose to Linda Bradley's face, and Martha suspected she was uncomfortable with what she was about to reveal. "Hank 'fessed up last night. He said he'd looked through Tom's pictures a couple of times, looking for photos of Anna. He must have knocked this one off the table."

Martha wondered which photograph Linda Bradley held so tightly. It must not be one of Anna, or Hank Bradley would have destroyed it.

"If I can't send it to Tom, you might as well have it," Tom's former landlady said at last, "seeing as it's of you."

As Linda Bradley turned the paper so that she could see it, Martha gasped. She had never believed in miracles, but this was as close to one as anything she'd experienced. The photograph Mrs. Bradley had found was the Fourth of July Woman.

"Thank you, Mrs. Bradley." Martha's hands were shaking with excitement as she reached for the photograph. "I know exactly what to do with this."

He had thought it would get easier. He had thought that the emptiness would fade, that his heart would accept what his mind knew, that leaving Canela was the best thing— the only thing—he could do. It had been three weeks. Surely by now the pain should have dissipated. Surely by now he should be enjoying life again. Instead, he was sitting in a restaurant, staring at the menu as if it were printed in a foreign language, unable to make a simple decision about what to order.

The waitress was young and attractive. Three months

ago, he would have flirted with her. Today Tom could not muster enough energy to smile.

"You look like you've lost your best friend," the young woman said as she approached the table to take his order.

"That's not far from the truth," Tom admitted. It was annoying that his feelings were so obvious, but what could he do? Though he'd tried to force a smile, that hadn't worked.

"Then I suggest you order the Salisbury steak and mashed potatoes." The waitress nodded as if her pronouncement were of earth-shaking importance. "It works every time."

"Let's give it a try." Tom doubted something as simple as food would have any effect, but he needed to eat. It might as well be Salisbury steak and mashed potatoes.

When the food arrived, Tom took a bite. The meat was hot and flavorful, but it made no difference. Nothing did. He was doing the same things he'd done for years, wandering from place to place, taking photographs, meeting people. The places were beautiful. He had the photographs to prove that. The people were friendly. He had photographs of them, too. Nothing had changed, and yet everything had. In the past, he had found pleasure in his travels. Each day had been an adventure, wondering what he would find around the next bend of the road or in the next town. Now the simple act of waking up felt like a chore. All of the zest was gone from his life, leaving him empty.

The reason wasn't difficult to find. He missed Martha. Without her, nothing mattered. He didn't even care that Sidney would fire him the next time he set foot in the *Gazette*'s offices. How could he care about his career or the money that it brought him when there was no one to share his success?

Tom swallowed another bite of meat, washing it down with a sip of iced tea. Though the waitress had recommended lemonade, Tom hadn't agreed to that. He hadn't drunk lemonade since he'd left Canela, and he doubted he ever would. Lemonade reminded him of the picnic in the bluebonnets and of how sweet Martha's kiss had been. Lemonade reminded him of how they'd laughed at the thunder and how, for a few moments, his life had felt complete. Those moments would never return, and only a fool would torture himself with memories of things that could not be repeated.

He missed Martha. He missed his conversations with Mr. Martin. He even missed the way the school children used to wave at him whenever they saw him. The truth was, though he had once thought it impossible, Tom missed Canela. He missed walking down Main Street. He missed—

As he poured gravy over a piece of meat, his hand stilled. That was it! That was the answer.

He rose and approached the waitress. "May I use your phone?"

It was the last day of school. The children fairly scampered with delight as they left the classroom, waving goodbye to Martha as if they would not encounter her on the streets of Canela during the summer recess and as if they wouldn't see her at the town's Fourth of July celebration. The children were happy and filled with excitement. She was unhappy and filled with nothing but regrets.

Martha could not remember a time in her life when she had felt so empty. When Henry had been killed, she had filled her days with teaching and caring for her siblings. Now there was nothing to look forward to, no reason to climb out of bed each morning. She had lost something infinitely precious, and it was her fault.

As she placed the last of the books on the shelf, Martha closed her eyes, remembering. It didn't matter where she went. Each street in Canela held memories of Tom. She could picture him setting up his tripod and photographing the bank. Other times, she remembered the afternoon they had visited Bertha Wilson and how wonderful it had felt holding baby Hannah. Most of all, Martha remembered the day they had traveled outside Canela to see the wildflowers.

Though the bluebonnets had long since faded, Martha could not forget the picnic she and Tom had shared or the way he'd laughed at the thunder. For days afterward, when she had thought of that day, Martha's memories had focused on Tom's kiss. It had been so sweet and tender that she knew she would never forget it. But today it was Tom's words that reverberated in her head. "No matter how bad things seem, something good will come from them," he had said, "if only you look for it."

Martha hadn't believed him. She had thought he was an idealist when he'd said that good could come from even the worst events. She took a deep breath and stared out the window at the oak tree where Tom had waited for her so many times. He was right. Horrible things had happened, but Tom was right. They had led to good. It was Martha who had been wrong, for she had not searched for the silver lining, she had not laughed at the thunder.

She gripped the windowsill, thinking about what had happened. Hank Bradley's snooping through Tom's pictures was wrong. The man should have respected Tom's privacy. But because he hadn't, there was still a print of Tom's Fourth of July Woman, and that was good. If everything went as Martha hoped it would, the photograph would save Tom's career. The men in the trenches would have the picture Tom believed so important, and the rest of the country would have many more years to enjoy Tom's poignant photos.

The fire that had destroyed Anna's house was the worst thing that had ever happened in Canela. If she could turn back time and keep the fire from being set, Martha would. Changing history was not within her power. Recognizing that the aftermath was positive was. Though she could never have predicted it, somehow the fire had served as a catalyst, bringing the townspeople together in a way that was unprecedented in Canela's history. Rivalries seemed, if not forgotten, at least put aside as the town rallied around Anna. Everyone had done something to make Anna realize that she was a valued member of the town, no matter where she had been born. Hank Bradley had even greeted her politely last week. That was, in Martha's opinion, a minor miracle.

She stepped away from the window and looked around the classroom. There was nothing left to do here. It was time to return home. Tomorrow she would meet with the Ladies' Auxiliary to finalize their plans for the Fourth of July celebration. Mrs. Bleeker and Mrs. Lewis would argue, as they always did, leaving Miss Bloom to play peacemaker.

Martha smiled as she realized that even Tom's leaving, as painful as it had been, had served a purpose. His accusations had made her face the truth. Tom was right. The town she loved wasn't perfect. He was also right that Martha had been wearing rose-colored glasses. She hadn't wanted to admit that her hometown was like every other one, that it held both good and bad. It had taken Tom to make Martha realize that Canela didn't have to be perfect. She could love it, despite its flaws.

She shut the school door behind her and walked down the steps, her left hand gripping the railing. As sun glinted off the gold band that Henry had placed on her third finger, Martha blinked. Was Tom right about that too? Had she been deluding herself, thinking that her marriage to Henry had been perfect? She twisted the ring. Though she had never removed it from her finger, she knew what was engraved inside it. Henry had chosen the same saying that Abraham Lincoln had put inside his wife's wedding band, *Love is eternal.*

Her legs suddenly weak, Martha sat down on the stairs and tried to slow the pounding of her heart. That wasn't a lie. Love *was* eternal. She loved Henry, and she knew that he had loved her. But, a little voice inside her said, theirs hadn't been a perfect marriage. It hadn't been like her parents' marriage. Everyone knew that, although they loved their children dearly, her parents' love for each other was the strongest, most important part of their lives. It hadn't been that way with Martha and Henry. Even after they'd married, Martha had continued to worry about her siblings, to put their needs ahead of her own and Henry's. And Henry had continued to be closer to his cousins in Canada than to her. That was why he had enlisted along with them.

Martha took a deep breath, exhaling slowly. Tom was right. Though she might not laugh at the thunder, she now accepted his belief that things—even bad things—happened for a reason. Everything that had happened in her life had been leading to this moment. Henry's death had forced her to be strong and to build her own life. Her siblings' leaving Canela had freed her from the responsibility she felt toward them. The fire that had destroyed Anna's house had taught Martha to view things as they really were, not as she wanted them to be.

She twisted her ring again. She loved Henry, and she always would. He would always be a part of her life, a key part of her childhood and early adulthood. That love was eternal. Martha knew that, just as she knew that while she had loved Henry, she had never been in love with him.

She stared at her wedding ring, trying to make sense of the emotions that were bombarding her. Tom. It all came back to Tom. Martha closed her eyes for a second, picturing him in the bluebonnet field, remembering how he had walked at her side so many days after school, thinking of the night he'd asked her to marry him. She had been wrong—so very, very wrong—to refuse him. She had let her fear of change overrule what her heart had told her. She had denied the truth that was now so evident. What

Martha felt for Tom was stronger and deeper than any emotion she had ever before experienced.

She loved Tom. She had admitted that to herself and to Anna. What she hadn't admitted was that she was in love with Tom. That was the difference. That was why she felt so bereft without him. That was why her life had lost its zest. Because she was in love with Tom, Martha wanted to be with him. She shook her head. It wasn't simply that she *wanted* to be with Tom. She *needed* to be with him if she was to be happy again. Martha rose and headed for home, her stride once more filled with confidence. It might not be easy. She knew that. But she also knew that she would do anything, anything on earth, to be with the man she loved.

"Will you water my flowers while I'm gone?" Martha asked Anna an hour later.

Her friend raised an eyebrow. "You're going away?" When Martha nodded, Anna stared at her for a long moment. "Are you sure?"

"I'm more certain than I've ever been of anything." And, as she walked back to her house, Martha slid Henry's ring off her finger.

Two more days. Tom pressed the hand lever forward, urging the car to accelerate. Two days and he would be in Canela. He frowned. Couldn't this automotive masterpiece go any faster? Two days and he would know whether he had a chance at happiness. Two days and he would know whether Martha loved him.

Though he hated to stop, the rumbling of his stomach told Tom that it was time to eat. He wouldn't take the time to go to a restaurant. Instead, he'd buy a loaf of bread and some cheese in the next town. He hated every minute he spent outside the car, for that was a minute he wasn't spending with Martha. Reluctantly, Tom stopped the Model T in front of a general store. If he was fortunate, there would be no one else shopping at this time. He could be in and out in less than five minutes. Luck was not with him. Three people stood in line, waiting to pay for their purchases.

Tom took his place in the queue. While the shopkeeper discussed the weather with the first customer, Tom looked around, and as he did, his eye was caught by the newspaper display. No! It couldn't be!

Tom yanked a copy of the *Gainey Gazette* from the pile and stared at it, not believing what his mind had registered. Tom's Fourth of July Woman was on the cover of one of the country's most widely read weekly papers.

He swallowed deeply, trying to fight back his rage. How could Sidney have done it? Anger fiercer than any he'd ever known rushed through Tom with the force of a speeding train. How could Sidney have betrayed his trust? Though they'd had their disagreements over the years they'd worked together, Tom had always believed Sidney to be an honorable man. The latest issue of the *Gainey Gazette* proved how wrong Tom had been. If the man hadn't been hundreds of miles away, Tom would gladly have throttled him within an inch of his life. How could his editor have betrayed both him and Martha?

Tom shuddered, trying to imagine Martha's reaction. He had promised her, not just once but many times, that he would not use her photograph. What must she be thinking now, seeing her face on the cover of the *Gazette*? She must surely believe that Tom had broken his word. In all likelihood, her anger was as deep as his own.

How had it happened? Why had Sidney disregarded Tom's explicit instructions? Tom's mind whirled as he paid for his food and the newspapers.

"Beautiful woman." The shopkeeper grinned as he looked at the *Gainey Gazette*. Tom simply nodded.

Was it possible that the telegram had not been delivered and this was an innocent mistake? How Tom hoped that was the case! Nothing could undo the fact that Martha's picture was on display across the country, but perhaps if she knew how it had come to be, Martha would be more understanding. One thing Tom knew was that he could not face her until he had the answer. He looked at the large clock on the wall. Sidney would still be at the office. Tom would phone him, and within an hour, he would know how this horrible mistake had occurred.

But Tom had not reckoned on Sidney's obstinacy. "I'm sorry, Tom," the woman who answered the phone at the *Gazette*'s headquarters said. "Mr. Vesper says if you want to talk to him, you'll have to come here."

Though he was only two days from Canela, Tom turned the Model T and headed north.

Chapter Twelve

Martha stared in amazement as she stepped outside Grand Central Station. Nothing she had read, none of the pictures she had seen had prepared her for this. New York City was so much bigger, so much grander, so much *more* than she had dreamt. As she looked first one direction, then the other, along Park Avenue, it seemed that the city stretched forever. And the noise. Never before had Martha encountered dozens of automobiles, their horns urging horse drawn wagons and carriages to move more quickly, while pedestrians fought their way across crowded intersections, some muttering imprecations, others conversing as though oblivious to the cacophony that enveloped them.

Martha had thought that summers in Texas had taught her about heat. New York proved her wrong, for heat was different here. Instead of coming only from the sun, it radiated from the streets and buildings, blending the smells of animals with the sweeter scents of flowers and the distinctly pleasant aroma of freshly baked bread.

Martha couldn't help it. She grinned. New York was huge and noisy and crowded, and she loved it. There was something so vital about this city that she couldn't help smiling, and though she was tired from days of travel, her step was jaunty as she hailed a taxicab to take her to her hotel.

An hour later, she stood in the front office of the *Gainey Gazette*. As she had climbed the stairs, the enthusiasm that had propelled her along the streets of New York evaporated, replaced by apprehension. "May I speak to Mr. Vesper?" Perhaps it was foolish, but Martha hadn't told Tom's editor that she was coming. When she had decided to make the journey, all that mattered was coming to New York and finding Tom. She hadn't considered that Sidney Vesper might be away. She hadn't considered that, even if he was here, he might not divulge Tom's address. As doubts assailed her, Martha felt her palms grow moist inside her gloves.

The clerk looked up at her. "Whom should I say . . . ?" The woman's words trailed off and her eyes widened. Wordlessly, she rose and opened one of the doors behind her. "Mr. Vesper, the Fourth of July Woman is here."

Seconds later the man Martha had traveled so far to see stood in the doorway. For an instant, Martha felt a sense of disappointment. She had expected Tom's editor to be bigger, taller, more impressive. Instead, he was a slight man, his dark hair showing a few threads of silver, his eyes partially hidden behind thick spectacles.

"Come in, Miss York."

"How did you know my name?" When she had sent the photograph to him, although she had signed the letter, she had not told Sidney Vesper that she was the subject of the photograph. She had simply said that this was Tom's picture of the Fourth of July Woman.

"Lucky guess." The editor gestured toward one of the chairs in front of his desk. Though the desk was covered with sheets of paper in what appeared to be total disorganization, the rest of the office was meticulously neat. Despite the open window, there was no trace of dust on the filing cabinets, and the potted plant that graced one corner boasted leaves so shiny that Martha wondered whether someone had polished them along with the furniture. "Please be seated, Miss York."

"It's Mrs. York." Though she had signed her letter *Mrs. Henry York* as she always did, it appeared that Mr. Vesper had not remembered that. Judging from the state of his desk, he received a large volume of correspondence and could hardly be expected to remember a detail from one piece.

As she took the seat he'd offered, Martha removed her gloves. The man gave her bare left hand a significant look.

"I'm a widow." Though she had once thought it unlikely, it no longer hurt to say those words, just as it no longer felt odd not to be wearing Henry's ring.

Sidney Vesper took his seat behind the desk, then leaned forward. "I'm sorry for your loss, Mrs. York, but I doubt you came all the way from Canela, Texas to tell me about it."

Martha took a deep breath, trying to quell the butterflies that were beating inside her stomach. Tom's editor appeared to be a reasonable man. Surely he would help her when he heard what she needed. "I came because I wanted to find Tom Fleming." By some small miracle, her voice did not betray her nervousness. "I thought he might be here."

The smile that crossed the editor's face held a hint of mischief. "We don't see him very often, but I imagine that will change once he sees the current issue of the *Gazette*."

"Then you printed the photo." Even though Sidney had insisted that the Fourth of July Woman's photograph was important to the *Gazette,* Martha hadn't been certain they would use it.

He nodded. "Not only did we print it, we used it for the cover."

Martha felt the blood drain from her face, and the butterflies resumed their churning. She had never considered that possibility. When Tom had spoken of the Fourth of July Woman, Martha had envisioned the photograph being hidden somewhere inside the magazine, one of the three or four pictures that formed a normal rotogravure page.

"I'm not sure how I feel about that."

"You should be honored. Only the very best photographs are good enough for the cover of the *Gainey Gazette*." Sidney turned and pulled a copy from the table behind him. As he handed it to Martha, he said, "This is the finest work Tom's ever done."

Martha stared at her photograph. Was that really her face? Somehow, it looked different in the brown tone of the rotogravure. Those were her eyes and nose, but the smile wasn't the way she remembered it. It was softer than she recalled, not mysterious like Mona Lisa, but almost dreamy. Martha studied the cover of the *Gainey Gazette*. The woman who bore an uncanny resemblance to her appeared to be a woman in love, a woman who was waiting for her man, a woman who would wait forever for the man she loved.

With shaking fingers, Martha laid the rotogravure on Sidney's desk. Was it true? Had she been in love with Tom from the very beginning? She no longer denied the fact that she loved Tom and that she was in love with him, but she hadn't realized she'd fallen in love so early. The cover of the *Gainey Gazette* said she had. Cameras, Tom had told her, didn't lie.

"Tom claimed it was his best," Martha admitted, "but I didn't see anything special in this picture." Talking about the picture was safer than considering the state of her heart.

This time there was no doubt that Sidney was amused. "The subject rarely sees a photograph the way the rest of us do. Tom was right, though. This was what the *Gazette* needed."

"Do you really believe Tom will come here?"

Nodding, Sidney said, "To tell you the truth, I'm surprised I haven't heard from him yet. This issue should have been in stores all across America yesterday. If I know him, and I think I do, Tom'll be madder than a hornet when he sees your picture."

"Will you let me speak to him if he phones?"

Sidney shook his head. "No."

That wasn't the response Martha had expected, and it certainly wasn't the one she wanted. "I need to talk to him. I need to explain."

"You need to talk to Tom. I need him to sign a new contract before *Life* or *The Saturday Evening Post* offers him something better." The editor gave Martha a conspiratorial smile. "It seems we both need Tom Fleming to come to New York."

Martha had accomplished everything she could today. As she started to rise, the clerk entered the office. "Mr. Vesper, Tom Fleming's phoned for you."

Sidney grinned, his smile saying "I told you so." "Tell Tom the only way I'll speak to him is if he comes here." When the young woman had left, Sidney nodded at Martha. "He'll be here within five days."

The next three days were the longest of Martha's life. She kept herself busy exploring the city, visiting the museums, the library, even going to Battery Park to admire the Statue of Liberty. The activities helped to pass the time, but try though she might, Martha could think of little other than the fact that soon she would see Tom. Soon she would know if he loved her. Soon she would know if they had a future together.

It was the morning of the fourth day, and Martha had come to the *Gainey Gazette* offices as she did twice each day. Sidney had told her that he expected to hear from Tom before he actually arrived in New York and had suggested that she stop in each morning and afternoon to see if Tom had phoned or sent a telegram. Though Martha knew that

Sidney was busy, he spent a few minutes with her each morning, suggesting places she might want to visit. She was seated in front of the editor's desk when they heard the outside door open.

"Where's Sidney?"

Martha's heart began to pound with excitement as she recognized Tom's voice. He was, as the editor had predicted, mad as a hornet whose nest had been disturbed. But what if Tom's anger was still directed towards her and not only at Sidney? Martha recoiled, and for a fleeting instant she regretted coming to New York. Then she reminded herself that only a coward would run away now. Martha might be foolish on occasions, she might be resistant to change, but she was not a coward. The moment of reckoning had arrived.

When Martha started to rise, Sidney shook his head. "Not yet." He mouthed the words, then walked to the door of his office, blocking the view of its interior.

"You got here faster than I expected. Looks like you just beat the storm." Sidney leaned against the doorframe, a man apparently at ease, a man who had nothing more serious to discuss than the dark clouds that were scudding across the sky.

"I would have been here sooner, but I had to replace the radiator." The weariness in Tom's voice wrenched Martha's heart. This was torture, listening to the man she loved but not being able to see him. She wanted to run to him, to put her arms around him and tell him that everything would be fine. Instead, she was trapped in front of a desk covered with tottering piles of paper.

"You must have been driving too many hours." Though Sidney's voice was devoid of inflection, Martha saw the corners of his mouth twitch. He was enjoying this.

Tom was not. Anger replaced weariness as he said, "I didn't come here to discuss the weather or automobile mechanics with you, Sidney. I want to know why you disregarded my instructions." There was a pause, then Tom continued, "I must have been mistaken when I thought you possessed some integrity."

Tom's editor's spine stiffened as the accusation hit. "Aren't you a little out of line here? You work for me." The hint of mirth had vanished. Sidney was all business.

"Not any longer. I won't work for a man who exposes an innocent woman to publicity she doesn't want." Though she could not see him, Martha heard Tom take a step forward. "I can't believe you did that, Sidney."

The editor shrugged, as if unfazed by Tom's anger. "You were right about the picture. It'll help boost the soldiers' morale. Besides," he said with a cynical smile, "it'll sell more copies. This is the best cover we've ever produced."

"Thanks to a picture you had no right to use. I told you specifically not to print any of my pictures of the blond woman. That one came to you by mistake."

The anguish in Tom's voice had Martha rising from her chair. She hadn't realized that Tom thought he'd somehow inadvertently sent her photograph to Sidney. Sidney shook his head slightly, telling Martha not to move. For some reason, the editor wasn't ready for Tom to know that she was here.

"I didn't use any that you sent me."

Tom's response was instantaneous. "I never thought you were a liar, but this cover says otherwise."

"Why is it so important to you?" Sidney demanded.

"Because unlike you, I value my integrity. I gave my word that I wouldn't use any photographs of her without her consent."

Martha could stand it no more. She took the three steps to the door and, as Sidney moved away, she faced Tom. "I gave my consent."

The man Martha loved more than anything on earth stared at her as if she were an apparition. "Martha! Why are you here?"

She couldn't tell him everything, not with Sidney and

the entire *Gainey Gazette* staff watching, and so she said only, "I've been waiting for you."

Apparently satisfied that he'd done his part, Sidney ushered Tom into his office, then closed the door, leaving Tom and Martha alone. By unspoken consent, they moved a few feet from the door and stood next to the window.

"I don't understand." Tom's face still registered shock. "Why did you come?"

"I didn't know how to reach you." She would tell him the easy part first. Martha owed Tom an apology. Only when that had been delivered would she admit to the other reason she had traveled so far. "I felt so badly about the things I said to you that last morning. I couldn't go through the rest of my life without apologizing to you."

Confusion clouded those dark blue eyes that had haunted so many of Martha's dreams. "But you hate traveling. You told me that."

"I also told you that I wouldn't let you use a photograph of me. That was before I knew how important it was for your career. I couldn't let you destroy your future just because I was being stubborn."

As the sun emerged from the clouds, a ray of sunshine spilled into the room. Tom blinked at the sudden brightness. "You didn't believe me when I told you it was important. What happened?"

Martha explained how she had phoned Tom's editor and what he had said. "Sidney had no right," Tom muttered.

"I'm glad he told me," she countered. "At first it made me feel more guilty for tearing up the copy you gave me, but when Mrs. Bradley found the other one under the bureau, I knew what I had to do."

Tom laid his hand on the windowsill, as if to steady himself. The lines of fatigue that etched his face bore mute witness to the days he'd driven so that he could confront his editor. "Then Sidney wasn't lying. He didn't use a picture I sent him." Martha nodded in confirmation. "I still don't understand," Tom continued. "I can understand why you sent Sidney the photograph. You're a kind woman, and you wanted to help. But why did you come all this way when you hate to travel? You could have sent a letter."

Martha took a deep breath and mustered every ounce of courage she possessed. This was the reason she had come to New York. This was the moment she had waited for. This was her chance at happiness, if only she dared bare her heart. It wasn't the way she had pictured it. When she had imagined the scene, Martha had thought they would go to one of the parks, perhaps Central Park. Not once had she considered that she would utter the most important words of her life in a newspaper office.

Martha took another breath, then swallowed. "I love you, Tom," she said firmly. "I would go to the ends of the earth for you."

The look of wonder that crossed his face made Martha's heart begin to pound. Perhaps Anna was right. Perhaps Tom did love her.

"Do you love me enough that you would stay in Canela?" he asked.

Stay in Canela? What did he mean? Was this Tom's way of saying that he didn't love her, that he regretted his proposal, that he had realized they had no future together? "I don't understand."

Tom took a step forward and reached for her hands. His were as warm and comforting as the smile he gave her. Surely he wasn't going to reject her, not with a smile like that. "You're not the only one who's been thinking about that day and who regrets what he said." Tom's voice was low but firm, and the warmth she saw in his eyes kindled a flame deep inside Martha.

"Anger kept me going for the first few days, but then I realized that traveling had lost its appeal." Martha felt her eyes widen in surprise. She had changed—she knew that she had—but she had not believed anything could cause such a fundamental change in Tom.

"Every time I entered a new town, I wished it were Canela." The flame inside Martha became a blaze. "Every time I walked down a strange street, I wished I were walking home from school with you. Every night, when I searched for something to do, I wished we were sitting on your front porch."

Dimly, Martha was aware that the room had grown darker, that clouds had obscured the sun. Dimly she heard a telephone ring and people speaking. None of that mattered. All that was important was Tom and the love she felt for him.

He tightened the grip on her hands. "I know you told me never to ask again, but I have to know if you've changed your mind. Will you marry me, Martha? Will you spend the rest of your life with me?"

Flames of happiness threatened to engulf her. Marrying Tom and staying in Canela would be the perfect life for Martha, a dream come true. There was nothing she wanted more, except to make Tom happy. No matter what it cost, she couldn't let him sacrifice his happiness for her. "What will you do?" she asked. "Photography is your life."

Tom nodded slowly, his expression serious. "It is," he agreed. "I can't imagine a life without photography any more than I can imagine a life without you." Tom's smile was the sweetest thing Martha had ever seen. It made her believe that maybe, just maybe, there would be a happy ending for her and Tom. "One of the things I realized after I left you is that I don't have to be the Peripatetic Photographer to have a fulfilling career. As I drove, I remembered the children's enthusiasm the day I spoke to them and the fact that there hasn't been a photographer in Canela for over ten years. I also remembered that there's going to be an empty store on Main Street." The enthusiasm in Tom's voice told Martha that this was something he'd considered carefully and that he liked his plans.

"I phoned Mr. Martin, and he agreed to rent me the store as soon as the Dress Emporium closes. Unless you object, I'm going to open a photography studio. I'll do the normal things that a photographer does, pictures of weddings and special occasions. But I'm also going to teach children how to take photographs. And"—Tom's eyes were serious as he looked at Martha—"if you agree, I'm going to spend a lot of time on that front porch with you." He glanced down at their clasped hands. When he raised his eyes again, there was a twinkle in them. "Maybe, if we're very lucky, some of those children I plan to teach will be ours."

The happiness that welled within Martha was deeper than anything she'd ever known. Marriage to Tom, having his children, raising them in the town she loved—it was everything Martha had ever wanted. "Are you sure this is what you want?"

Tom smiled. "I've never been so certain of anything." He paused for a second, and then he said the words she had longed to hear. "I love you, Martha, and I want to marry you." Tom dropped to his knees and looked up at her. "Will you be my wife?" He reached into his pocket and pulled out a small box that could hold only one thing. "This belonged to my grandmother," Tom said as he opened the box, revealing a diamond in an antique filigree setting. "If you want a new ring, we'll go to Tiffany's this afternoon, but it's been Fleming family tradition that this ring goes to the first bride of each generation."

Martha smiled. "You know I love tradition."

His eyes twinkling again, Tom looked up at her. "Does that mean you'll marry me?"

"Oh, yes, my love."

Tom slid the ring on her finger. "I love you, Martha, and I'll do everything I can to make you happy." He paused, and his face was solemn as he said, "I won't try to take Henry's place or destroy his memory."

Martha tugged on Tom's hands. It was vital that he understood how she felt. They couldn't begin a life together with shadows between them. When Tom was standing, Martha leaned forward and pressed a kiss on his lips. "I loved Henry," she said, "and I always will. He'll always have a place in my heart, just as my family does." She squeezed Tom's hand, relishing the sensation of having his ring on her finger. "My love for you is different. The truth is, I've never loved anyone the way I love you, and I know I'll never love this way again." Martha smiled at the happiness she saw shining from Tom's eyes. "I'm in love with you, Tom. I want to be your wife and to spend the rest of my life making you happy."

The smile he gave her told Martha that Tom understood. They both knew that life brought no guarantees, but that same experience had taught them to enjoy each moment and to cling to happiness.

"I love you, Martha." As Tom drew her into his arms and she raised her lips for his kiss, a bolt of lightning split the sky. A second later, thunder rolled and a deluge of rain beat against the window. For a second Tom and Martha stared at each other. Then, in unison, they began to laugh.

Dear Reader,

I hope you enjoyed Martha and Tom's story and that you've had as much fun as I have with the Wentworth sisters. I thoroughly enjoyed getting to know them and bringing them to life for you.

If this is your first War Brides Romance, you may have wondered about Martha's sisters. Carolyn is the Wentworth daughter who's cap-over-boots in love with her new husband. Even Martha doesn't know the whole story of how Carolyn met him and the obstacles she had to overcome before she found her happy ending. Then there's Emily, the plucky sister who travels to France and braves the dangers of the war zone to find her brother. Along the way, Emily discovers a temperamental Model T, a scruffy dog, and a man who brings her much more than she expects, including her own chance at love.

Dancing in the Rain, *which tells Carolyn's story,* and Emily's story, Whistling in the Dark, *are currently available. If you haven't read them, I hope you will.*

Happy reading,
Amanda Harte